Kensy and Max Books

Jacqueline Harvey

KENSY AND MAX

BREAKING NEWS

Kane Miller
A DIVISION OF EDC PUBLISHING

First American Edition 2020
Kane Miller, A Division of EDC Publishing

First published Random House Australia in 2018,
Penguin Random House Australia Pty Ltd.
Copyright © Jacqueline Harvey 2018
The moral right of the author has been asserted.

For information contact:
Kane Miller, A Division of EDC Publishing
P.O. Box 470663
Tulsa, OK 74147-0663
www.kanemiller.com
www.edcpub.com
www.usbornebooksandmore.com

Library of Congress Control Number: 2019940408

Printed and bound in the United States of America
1 2 3 4 5 6 7 8 9 10
ISBN: 978-1-61067-992-3

For Ian

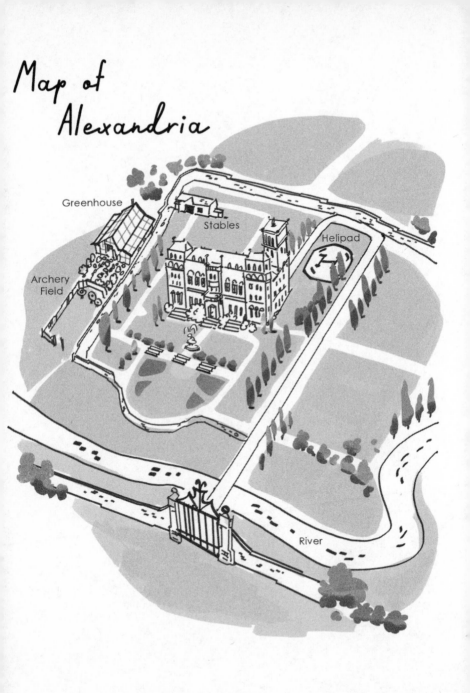

Map of Millbank

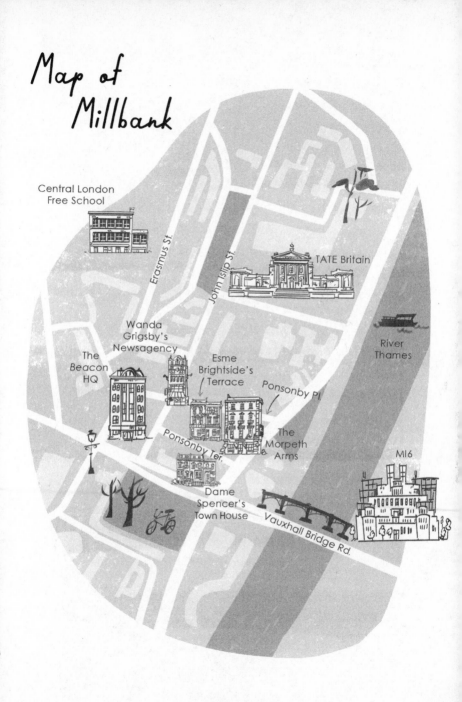

Central London Free School

Erasmus St.

John Islip St.

TATE Britain

Wanda Grigsby's Newsagency

The Beacon HQ

Esme Brightside's Terrace

Ponsonby Pl.

River Thames

Ponsonby Ter.

The Morpeth Arms

MI6

Dame Spencer's Town House

Vauxhall Bridge Rd.

CAST OF CHARACTERS

The Grey household

Kensington Méribel Grey	11-year-old twin
Maxim Val d'Isère Grey	11-year-old twin
Anna Grey	Kensy and Max's mother
Edward Grey	Kensy and Max's father
Fitzgerald Williams	Kensy and Max's manny, best friend of Edward Grey

Alexandria Estate

Dame Cordelia Spencer	Owner of Alexandria
Wellington and Mackintosh	Dame Spencer's West Highland terriers
Song	Butler
Mim	Head gardener

Chester	Pet squirrel
Shugs	Gardener
Mr. O'Leary	Gardener
Ida Thornthwaite	Cook

Central London Free School staff

Magoo MacGregor	Headmaster
Daphne Potts	Personal assistant to the headmaster
Romilly Vanden Boom	Science teacher
Monty Reffell	History teacher
Willow Witherbee	English teacher
Cosette Verte	Languages teacher
Elliot Frizzle	Art teacher
Lottie Ziegler	Mathematics teacher
Gordon Nutting	PE teacher
Elva Trimm	Head dinner lady
Eric Lazenby	Custodian

Central London Free School students

Autumn Lee, Harper Ballantine, Carlos Rodriguez, Sachin Varma, Yasmina Ahmed, Dante Moretti, Inez Dufour	Kensy and Max's friends
Amelie Jagger	Older girl
Alfie	Boy in Lower Sixth

| Lola Lemmler | Unfriendly girl, especially to new students |
| Misha Thornhill | Lola's friend |

Residents of Millbank

Wanda Grigsby	Owner of the corner shop in Ponsonby Place
Derek Grigsby	Wanda's son
Esme Brightside	Friend of Wanda and Ivy
Ivy Daggett	Friend of Wanda and Esme
Claudia	Neighbor in Ponsonby Terrace
Gary	Manager of The Morpeth Arms
Stephie	Bar attendant at The Morpeth Arms

Other

| Sidney | Butler |

CHAPTER 1

BKDIXKA

Max woke with a start as the car crunched to a halt. He yawned and looked around at his sister, who was still asleep in the back seat. Her blanket had slipped down and she was drooling on the pillow that was wedged in the corner. She wouldn't thank him for noticing.

The boy peered out at the jewel box of stars in the clearing night sky. It had only stopped raining a little while ago. On the other side of the car, Max could see what looked to be a hotel. A dull glow shone from one of the windows high in the roofline. For a second, he glimpsed a face, but it was gone as soon as it had appeared. "Where are we, Fitz?" Max asked.

Fitz turned and gave him a weary smile. "This is Alexandria," he replied, as if that was supposed to mean something. "Be a good lad and take the daypacks with you, and mind the puddles. No one will thank you for tramping mud inside."

Fitz opened the driver's door and hopped out of the Range Rover.

Max stretched, yawning again, then reached over and gently shook his sister's leg. "Kensy," he whispered, "we're here."

The girl groaned and flopped her head against the pillow but didn't wake up. It was to be expected given they'd just spent the past sixteen hours driving from Zermatt, near the Swiss–Italian border, across France and then to England.

Fitz reappeared at the open driver's window. "Don't wake your sister unless you want your head bitten off," he warned with a wink.

Kensy let out a grunty snore, as if to agree.

Max heard footsteps on the gravel and looked up to see a tall man approaching. The fellow was wearing a red dressing gown and matching slippers. His dark hair had retreated to the middle of his head and he sported large rimless glasses. Fitz walked toward him and the two shook hands.

As the men spoke in hushed tones, the boy slipped out of the car. The stars had disappeared again and fat drops of rain began splattering the driveway. Max quickly collected the packs from the back seat while the man in the dressing gown retrieved their suitcases from the trunk. Fitz swept Kensy into his arms and carried her through a stone portico to an open doorway.

"Are we home?" she murmured, burrowing into the man's broad chest.

"Yes, sweetheart," he replied. "We're home."

Max felt a shiver run down his spine. He wondered why Fitz would lie. This wasn't their home at all.

The four of them entered the building into a dimly lit hallway. Without hesitation or instruction, Fitz turned and continued up a staircase to the right.

That's strange, Max thought. Fitz must have been here before.

"Please go ahead, Master Maxim," the tall man said.

Too tired to ask how the fellow knew his name, Max did as he was bid. The hypnotic thudding of their luggage being carried up the stairs made the boy feel as if he was almost sleepwalking. They followed Fitz down a long corridor and eventually came to a bedroom furnished with two queen-sized beds and a fireplace. Max's skin tingled from the warmth of the crackling fire. He deposited the daypacks neatly by the door and shrugged off his jacket as the tall man set down their bags and drew the curtains.

"Sweet dreams, Kens," Fitz whispered, tucking the girl under the covers.

Without any urging at all, Max climbed into the other bed. He had so many questions, but right now he couldn't muster a single word. The soft sheets and the thrum of driving rain against the windowpanes made it hard to resist the pull of sleep. He closed his eyes as Fitz and the tall man began talking. Max roused at the mention of his parents' names followed by something rather alarming – something that couldn't possibly be true. He tried hard to fight off the sandman to hear more, but seconds later Max too was fast asleep.

CHAPTER 2

ILZHBA FK

Kensy scraped her hair into a ponytail and sat down at the end of the bed to put on her shoes. Somewhere in the building, a grandfather clock began to chime. She counted the bells in her head and was surprised to discover how late it was. She'd been up for ages and had attempted to wake Max a couple of times already, but it seemed the boy could sleep through an earthquake this morning.

Unlike her brother, who was usually a light sleeper and early riser, Kensy only had two speeds – full tilt and out cold. The second she was awake, Kensy needed to get out there and be amongst it, wherever "it" happened to be. Right at that moment the girl couldn't wait a minute longer. She marched over to pull back the heavy brocade drapes, flooding the enormous room with sunlight.

"No way!" she breathed, her green eyes the size of dinner plates.

Kensy quickly unlatched the window and swung it open, drinking in the view. Directly below her was a red gravel pathway and, beyond that, a gigantic fountain surrounded by low hedges laid out in a geometrical pattern. Trees resembling oversized lollipops stood in a line along the top terrace. On another level, accessed by one of at least three sets of stone steps, were flower beds still in bloom. Past the garden were rolling green fields dotted with frothy white sheep, and a shimmering river meandered through it all. Over to the right, Kensy could see a high stone wall and, to the left of the main drive, a thick woodland. She thought the scene looked more like a painting than real life and it was all just begging to be explored.

"Okay, that's it." Kensy shut the window, then slid across the polished floorboards and leapt onto her brother's bed. "Max!" she said, jumping up and down. "You have got to see this!"

The boy rolled away and pulled the covers over his head.

"This place is incredible! The garden – it's gorgeous – not to mention that you could do laps in the bathtub. Mum would love it," Kensy prattled, her words tumbling out like a waterfall. "Anyway, you need to get up. I'm starving . . . and someone has locked us in our room."

Max resurfaced, pushing himself up against the cloud of pillows. "What do you mean we're locked in?" he yawned. The door was probably just stuck. His sister was prone to exaggeration and enjoyed nothing more than to imagine the most outlandish scenarios for which there was usually a perfectly rational explanation.

"I mean exactly what I said," Kensy replied, continuing to jump. "The handle won't budge. Seriously, who locks a door from the outside? What if there was a fire? I have half a mind to call the concierge and give them an earful. And where is Fitz? He never lets us sleep in this late. It's after nine o'clock."

Max frowned and reached for his spectacles. His sister's suitcase had already exploded halfway across the room. Although it came as no surprise, it still bothered him. Max hopped out of bed and sidestepped a pile of underwear, resisting the urge to tidy the mess. "I'm having a shower first, then I'll deal with the locked door," he said, grabbing some clean clothes and his toiletries bag. "And can you *not* jump on my bed with your shoes on?"

Kensy fell back onto the duvet with an exasperated groan. Her brother always took *forever* to get ready, which was probably why he *always* looked as if he had stepped straight from the pages of a magazine, while Kensy mostly looked as if she'd been dragged through a bush backward. It went without saying that Max took after their mother, who often gently suggested that her daughter should become better acquainted with a hairbrush.

Kensy leapt up and consoled herself by

hunting around the bedroom for a solution. She tried the two mahogany armoires first, then the bedside cabinets, the fancy inlaid dressing table and, lastly, felt around every single floorboard to see if any of them were secret compartments in disguise. When she didn't find what she was looking for, she barged into the bathroom as her brother was pulling on his shirt.

"Haven't you heard of knocking?" he grumbled.

"Since when do you care?" Kensy opened the top drawer of the vanity. She rattled around among the cotton swabs and bars of soap before locating her prize. "Excellent," she said, and charged back out the door.

Max sighed and hung up his sister's abandoned towel along with his own. He walked out of the bathroom to find Kensy crouching by the bedroom door. "What are you doing?" he asked, slipping on his shoes.

"What does it look like I'm doing, silly?" Kensy replied, her face inches from the door handle. "I'm picking the lock, just the way Fitz taught us."

Max watched as his sister set to work,

jiggling the pins inside the keyhole. He bent down to see if she was making any progress when, suddenly, there was a faint click.

"Voilà, little brother!" Kensy grinned and turned the handle. "No need for applause, just a 'Wow, you're the smartest, most incredible girl I know' will do."

Max rolled his eyes. "And modest too."

As Kensy darted into the hallway, Max hung back and looked left and right.

The passage played host to an array of antique furniture, with more side tables and mirrors than anyone would ever find useful as well as a grandfather clock in a burr walnut case. Max noticed a particularly tall lamp with a red shade that looked a lot like a skinny woman wearing an oversized hat. All was still but for the gentle swishing of the lampshade tassels. Max couldn't help wondering if the object had swiveled around of its own accord. He scratched his head – perhaps his sister's wild imagination was beginning to rub off on him. Clearly, the idea was preposterous.

"Hurry up," Kensy called.

Reluctantly, Max went after her. He had been keen to make further investigations of the lamp, but as always, his sister got her way. Max kept to the center of the wide Chinese carpet runner, which did nothing to mask the squeaky floorboards. The boy soon stopped again; a large dome sitting atop a cabinet had caught his attention. Kensy turned and walked back to see what he was gawping at this time.

"Well, that's disgusting," she said, eyeing the taxidermy weasel. It was sporting a look of unbridled glee and had a furry creature hanging limply from its mouth.

Max leaned in. "I think it's kind of interesting in a gross way. I'd love to know how they get the fur to shine like that."

"Eww," Kensy said, wrinkling her nose. She poked her tongue out at the beady-eyed beast and dashed off, as if the weasel might spring back to life.

The building was bathed in silence apart from the sound of their footsteps and the ticking of the clock, which presently announced the half hour.

"Don't you think it's weird there are no numbers on the doors?" Kensy asked, finally taking stock of their surroundings. "And it's dead quiet – where are all the guests?"

Max looked up and down the hallway. He'd had the same thought and had noticed there were no fire extinguishers or exit signs either, which did seem odd for a public establishment. "Maybe it's one of those exclusive lodges and it's low season?" the boy said.

"Gee, if a hotel as good as this can't get business, even in low season, then there wouldn't be much hope for the ordinary ones around here," Kensy mused.

They had reached a grand staircase that was at least eight feet wide and in possession of the most intricately carved balusters in the shape of lighthouses. Kensington ran her fingers around one of them.

"We need to find Fitz," Max said. "I've got to talk to him about something."

"Yes, like why we were locked in our room for a start," the girl said.

Max shook his head. "Not just that. Last

night I heard him talking to the fellow who carried our bags inside."

"So?" Kensy said.

"He mentioned something about Mum and Dad, except that he called them Anna and Ed." Max paused, unsure if he should tell his sister the rest.

"Well, what did he say?" Kensy asked. She had a knack for being able to tell when her brother was keeping something to himself.

Max swallowed hard. "That they're missing."

"Missing!" Kensy laughed. "They've just been delayed. It's not the first time it's happened. You know that as well as I do."

"Not like this," Max insisted, biting his bottom lip. "Think about it, Kens. For some reason unknown to us, Fitz drove us across *three* countries for hours on end and we haven't heard from Mum and Dad for three days."

Kensy felt a twinge in her stomach. It did seem strange when her brother put it like that. Their parents had been away for almost six weeks, having enjoyed a long-overdue holiday in the Maldives before traveling to Africa to work with a children's medical charity, and they were all due to be reunited yesterday. Kensy and Max were the ones who had convinced them to go in the first place, and their parents had only agreed because Fitz was there to look after the twins.

Their mother, a doctor, and their father, a paramedic, were both expert skiers and had fallen into a nomadic existence, working with ski patrols and in medical clinics in resorts all over the world. When the twins were born, Ed and Anna Grey didn't see any reason to change their way of life. Hence, the family never stayed more than six months in the same place. It was unconventional, but the twins wouldn't have swapped it for anything. The past year had seen the Greys and Fitz bounce between Cervinia in Italy, and Thredbo in Australia. Before that, they had enjoyed stints in Queenstown, New Zealand, and Whistler, Canada, as well as resorts in the United States and Japan.

"I don't believe you," Kensy said, turning her back to her brother. She gripped the banister and peered at the vestibule below. "You must have imagined it."

Max had initially thought the same thing, but he was more convinced than ever of what the man had said. He turned his attention to the portraits that lined the landing, as if they might hold the answer. But their vacant stares only looked through him. "I know what I heard, Kens," he said softly.

His sister huffed and pushed away from the rail. "You were probably sleepwalking or something silly like that. Mum and Dad are *fine*," she said, and flew down the staircase. "I *know* they are. You're just being horrible."

Max watched helplessly as she stormed toward the front door. "Where are you going?" he called.

"I need some air, and there's not enough out there for the both of us!" Kensy wrenched open the giant panel and thundered down the front steps. The door creaked to a close behind her.

"Fine," Max sighed. In his experience, it was best to leave his sister alone when she was upset. Besides, it would give him a chance to find Fitz and get to the bottom of what was really going on.

CHAPTER 3

QEB DXOABK

Kensy bristled as she ventured out into the chilly winter morning. There was something alive in the air – perhaps it was the smell of the sea. Her light cotton cardigan wasn't the best choice, but she'd rather freeze to death than be back inside with Max right now.

The fountain she'd spied from the window towered in front of her. It was even more impressive up close. Standing in the center of a pond that was bigger than the average swimming pool was a bronze statue of Atlas, a Titan in ancient Greek mythology, holding up the globe. Kensy knew exactly how he felt. Her brother's words had made her feel a little like she had the weight of the world on her shoulders too. She banished the thoughts from her mind and consoled herself with the knowledge that transport in central Africa was notoriously unreliable at the best of times.

Kensy hurried along a gravel path bordered by hedges so perfect she imagined they could have only been cut with a laser beam. She spun around to look at the mansion, its symmetry flawless but for a square tower that rose at the rear on the right-hand side. Kensy wondered what was up there. With double-height bay windows at either end, the building resembled something from a fairy tale, except at that very moment it gave her a horrible sense of fore-boding. Kensy shivered and rubbed her arms.

Breaking into a jog, the girl passed the pristine lawn and rows of manicured flower beds, which soon gave way to wildflowers and century-old trees just begging to be climbed. She thought how Max would love them too, then remembered she was supposed to *not* think about him. Kensy pushed the notion from her mind and snatched a couple of daisies that were poking untidily from a voluminous bush.

Directly ahead, she was confronted with a high stone wall covered in ivy. It seemed to go on forever, running perpendicular to the side of the main building and creating a dead end. Kensy was about to turn back when she heard voices on the other side of the wall. They belonged to two men. One fellow sounded as if he'd been gargling gravel while the other had a strong Irish accent. Intrigued, Kensy took a step closer.

"Do you think they'll be staying long?" the Irishman grunted before a loud, heavy thump shook the ground.

Leaves from a nearby oak tree fell in protest.

"I can't imagine it," the gravel-grinder replied, followed by another loud thud. "They say she's the image of ma'am in her younger years and he'd give a young Robert Redford a run for his money."

Kensy thought the men must have been carrying something awfully heavy to have made the ground tremble in that way. All sorts of possibilities flashed through her mind. Not one to be kept guessing, the girl swung herself up onto the lowest branch of the oak tree, but it was nowhere near high enough to see over the wall. Kensy reached through the leaves for another branch and almost lost her balance as it came away in her hand. She steadied herself and saw that she wasn't holding a twig at all. She had dislodged an arrow from the tree trunk. Upon closer inspection, it appeared as though the tip was covered in crusty blood. How odd. Kensy wondered about the poor creature that might have died at the end of it. She clutched her prize and studied the tree, looking for another route skyward. At least the men's voices were clearer from up there.

"When are you going down to London?" the Irishman asked.

"When I get word," the other fellow replied. "First, we have to deal with these bodies. Gawd blimey, this one's a brute."

Bodies! Kensy's hand flew to her mouth, stifling a gasp. The arrow fell silently to the ground.

"'Urry up, will ya? I need to get that fancy soil round to Mim or she'll be baying for my blood," said the man with the gravelly voice.

The two men grunted, as though lifting another sizeable weight, and another dull thud sounded.

"Rightio, I'd better attend to old Atlas," the Irishman said.

There was a scraping noise and a door in the wall below opened. Kensy hadn't even noticed it there, concealed as it was beneath the thick blanket of ivy. She flattened herself against the largest branch, hoping the man wouldn't look up.

"Oh, on second thoughts, I'd better go with you. I need the trailer," he said, and disappeared back through the secret door.

Kensy sighed with relief as she heard the bolt slide across. With her heart racing, she jumped down from the tree and ran along the wall toward the house, splashing through puddles in her haste. She wished she'd been able to get a look at the men so she could give the police a proper description. She was on the edge of the pathway that led back to the front of the house when she spotted another door. It was almost obscured but for the glint of a brass handle. Kensy made a dash for it – perhaps she could still catch a glimpse of them from a distance.

She wrenched open the door and charged through into a jungle. Kensy hadn't experienced humidity like this since her family was forced to make an unscheduled stopover in Singapore a couple of years ago. She took off her cardigan and tied it around her waist.

It seemed she'd stumbled upon a greenhouse. The high stone wall she'd just come through formed the back of it, but the rest of the elaborate structure was made entirely of glass, much like an ornate Victorian dollhouse. It appeared to house a vegetable patch the size of at least two tennis courts and a variety of plants – some she recognized and others that were completely unknown to her. Banana trees heaved under huge hands of fruit, and something that looked like strawberries flourished, except these were white with red seeds. There were bright-orange cubes that resembled pumpkins but for their square shape, as well as fruit she would have guessed to be avocados were it not for the fact they were glowing an iridescent yellow.

Unfortunately, there was no sign of the men, and as much as she was keen to explore, Kensy knew she had to find her way back to the house so she could tell Max what she'd heard. On her way out, she turned into another row and came across the most extraordinary-looking cherry tomatoes. They were plump and red with a purplish tinge to them. Unable to ignore her grumbling stomach, Kensy plucked one of the fruits and popped it into her mouth. A flavor like nothing she had ever experienced flooded her taste buds. It was tomato but with a burst of passion fruit.

"Spit that out!" a voice shrieked. "Spit it out NOW!"

Kensy almost jumped out of her skin. She looked up to see a woman hurtling toward her, waving a rake in the air as if she were about to swat her with it. Fearing the worst, Kensy spat the masticated red ball as far as she could. It landed with a splat on the woman's left cheek.

"I'm so sorry," Kensy squeaked, shielding herself from imminent attack.

The woman came to a screeching halt. She pulled a tissue from her pocket and calmly wiped the splodge from her face. "Oh, thank heavens for that."

"What's the matter with it?" Kensy asked, lowering her arms. She wiped her tongue on her sleeve to make sure there were no remnants of the suspect fruit, at the same time wishing she could have another bite.

"Nothing, I hope," the woman said. "They just haven't been tested yet and they were sprayed with organic fertilizer yesterday, straight from the dairy."

Kensy registered the woman's meaning and began wiping her tongue more vigorously.

Out of nowhere, a gray squirrel ran up the woman's back and sat twitching on top of her floppy straw hat.

"I'm sorry I startled you, Chester," the woman said, her voice softening. She reached into the front pocket of her overalls and held out an acorn. The creature grabbed it in both paws and began nibbling away.

Kensy was mesmerized, and for a moment all thoughts of murderers and missing parents had evaporated. "Is he your pet?" she asked.

"His mother was killed in a storm. I found the poor little fellow shaking in the bottom of a felled tree. I raised him, but he knows he's free to go anytime he likes," the woman explained. Perhaps it was the unruly gray plait that fell over her shoulder almost to her waist, or her kindly eyes, but something about her put Kensy at ease.

"I'm sorry about before," the girl said, smiling. "I've got to go and report a mur–"

Her words were drowned out by a loud whumping noise.

Kensy glanced up at the pitched glass roof as a helicopter rose into the sky. Painted on its underside was a lighthouse that was square at the base and circular up top. The helicopter hovered for a few seconds before it disappeared over the woodland and into the blue sky beyond.

"You must have some important guests

staying here," Kensy remarked. The only times she'd seen helicopters were during rescues on the ski slopes or in Queenstown, where there seemed to be as many helicopters as tourists some days. She'd seen people plucked off mountains in Canada and Switzerland and more recently in Australia, usually with a broken bone or two or sometimes worse.

The woman chortled. "No, dear, that's Cordelia. She *owns* Alexandria."

"Wow. It must be amazing to own a hotel." Kensy looked around the greenhouse, wondering what on earth a rich lady who owned a helicopter would want with all these vegetables. Perhaps she was some sort of fancy organic farmer. "If I were Cordelia, I'd eat my body weight at the breakfast buffet and would never make my bed ever again."

"That does sound devilishly good, but Alexandria is not . . ." The woman stopped, distracted by the squirrel scampering down from her hat to her shoulder.

In the distance, Kensy caught sight of a couple of chaps who had popped up at the other end of the garden. One was tall and broad shouldered while the other was thin and wiry. They were both wearing green coveralls and the shorter chap had a flat cap on his head. Kensy gasped, realizing they could be the men from before. Although, not having seen them, it was impossible to know for sure. They both turned and stared at her. She shifted uncomfortably from one leg to the other, debating whether to tell the woman what she'd overheard.

"I should go and find my brother," the girl said, deciding against it. She gave the woman a quick wave, then turned on her heel and hurried back to the door she'd come through. Kensy didn't see the men smile and wave, nor did she see the woman brush tears from her twinkling gray eyes.

"Oh, darling girl," the woman breathed, clasping her hands in front of her, "it's so good to have you home."

CHAPTER 4

XIBUXKAOFX

After almost an hour of wandering the halls, Max was yet to encounter a single soul. He had passed through sitting room after sitting room, each warmed by a crackling fire, and had even happened upon a grand dining room set for at least fifty guests. It was all rather eerie, especially with the faint twang of country music that was drifting from the air vents. Fitz was nowhere to be found either, and Max was beginning to wish he'd gone after his sister.

As for whether this place was actually a hotel, Kensy's theory was looking more plausible by the second. None of it added up. Max had happened upon a whole room dedicated to one hundred samurai swords (he'd counted them in his head). They were mostly sheathed and hanging on the walls, although there were several on display in a glass case alongside three full suits of samurai armor. If Kensy had been queasy about the weasel upstairs, she was definitely going to hate the billiard room, which, apart from boasting a magnificent full-sized table, played host to a comprehensive collection of antique hunting trophies. Max found them strangely fascinating and utterly repulsive at the same time. He couldn't help wondering if any of the poor creatures had acquired names during their residency. The Javan rhino over the fireplace looked like a Herbert to him.

Max's favorite room by far, however, was the library. He loved to read and this one had the most impressive collection he'd ever encountered. He had hesitated for a mere second before scurrying up one of two ladders that ran around the mahogany bookshelves on a well-oiled rail. From this vantage point, he spied works by the world's greatest authors. Dickens, Shakespeare, Austen and just about every other writer worth their salt lined the shelves.

When Max stumbled upon a copy of *Treasure Island*, the boy's mind turned to more sober thoughts. His parents had given him that book on his last birthday. What if something really had happened to them? He jumped to the floor and was about to leave when a particularly colorful cover caught his eye. It was displayed on a little brass stand beside a stripy armchair. Max picked it up and ran his fingers along the embossed title – *The Caesar Shift* – then thumbed through the first chapter. He loved codes and puzzles, so this was right up his alley. Max flicked back to the title page. Halfway down was a handwritten inscription, except that it too was in code:

QLLROPLKBAPLKQEBLZZXPFLK
LCVLROQEFOQBBKQEYFOQEAXV.
TBIZLJBQLQEBCFOJ.
TFQELRORKTXSBOFKDILSB
XKAXCCBZQFLK, Z & A

Max was keen to crack it and began hunting around for a piece of paper and a pen when there was a loud skirmish outside the room. He quickly returned the book to the stand. Seconds later, two West Highland terriers skittered into the library and danced at the boy's feet.

"Hello, where did you come from?" Max leaned down to give them a pat. He noticed they were wearing identical blue collars, both glittering with diamanté and a shiny name tag. Max peered at the first one. "Wellington. That's cute. And you are?" He reached for the other tag. "Mackintosh."

Max knelt on the floor as the dogs nuzzled and sniffed and lolled about.

"Wellie and Mac." The boy chuckled to himself. "Like gum boots and a raincoat."

"Ah, you have a masterful brain, Master Maxim," a man said.

Max looked up to find the fellow from the previous night standing before him. Only, this time he wasn't wearing his dressing gown and slippers. Instead, the man was immaculately dressed in a black tuxedo with shoes so highly polished Max could see his own reflection in them. The man smiled at him.

"H-hello," Max said, pushing up his spectacles. He scrambled to his feet. "I didn't mean to snoop about. I was looking for Fitz. Have you seen him? And have you seen my sister? She went for a walk in the garden."

Running feet thudded in the hallway.

"That will be Miss Kensington now," the man said. He turned toward the door just as the girl ran past.

The sound of her sneakers skidding on the floorboards caused them both to wince, before she doubled back and appeared in the doorway. The girl was quite a sight to behold with her flushed cheeks, muddied jeans and her wild hair speckled with leaves. Max was puzzled to see that his sister had her cardigan tied around her waist on a chilly autumn day.

"Max!" Kensy exclaimed breathlessly. "I've been looking everywhere for you. I met this lady with a pet squirrel! And I found a green-house with tomatoes that taste like passion fruit. And there were two men who said something about getting rid of bod–" She stopped abruptly when she realized they had company.

"Good morning, Miss Kensington," the man in the tuxedo said pleasantly. "I was just coming to find you and Master Maxim for breakfast. Although, perhaps at this time of the morning, we should call it brunch."

The man bowed deeply as the girl hurried to her brother's side. The two dogs had scampered around behind the fellow and were now sitting at attention.

"How do you know our names?" Kensy asked, as the thought also formed in Max's head. He vaguely remembered thinking the same thing last night, when they'd arrived.

The man's dark eyes twinkled. "Forgive me. I am Song, and it is a pleasure to make your acquaintances." He bowed once more. "I am your butler."

The twins glanced at each other, then turned back to Song.

"For the hotel, you mean?" Kensy said, a crease forming on her forehead.

Song grinned. "Alexandria is not a hotel,

although I can understand how you reached such a conclusion."

"So, you're a servant?" Max asked. He wondered if they'd somehow traveled back in time.

Kensy scoffed. "Isn't that against the law these days?"

"I am a butler, Master Maxim, Miss Kensington, not a servant. Confucius says choose a job you love and you will never have to work a day in your life. I can assure you that *I* have never worked a day in my life," Song said with a satisfied nod.

"What's he talking about?" Kensy whispered to her brother. "What confusion?"

"It's Confucius," Max explained. "He was an ancient Chinese philosopher, and what Song is saying is that he loves his job, so it doesn't feel like work to him. That still doesn't explain whose house this is."

"Oh, it's Cordelia's," Kensy said. "The lady with the pet squirrel said so. She flew off in a helicopter a little while ago. Cordelia – not the lady with the pet squirrel."

At the mention of the woman's name, the two dogs began to wag their tails.

"Yes, Dame Spencer is mistress of the estate," Song said, nodding. "Now, Mr. Fitz has had some business to attend to, so if you would be kind enough to accompany me to the conservatory, I have arranged creamy scrambled eggs on toast for you, Miss Kensington, and fried eggs with crispy bacon and a well-cooked tomato for you, Master Maxim."

The twins exchanged looks of mild alarm. Those dishes were recent favorites which Fitz usually cooked for Sunday breakfast.

"Well . . . I am starving," Max said. His stomach growled for the umpteenth time that morning.

"Me too," Kensy agreed.

Song bowed again. "Then, without further ado, please follow me."

Kensy was disappointed to see the two dogs trotting off in the opposite direction.

"I wish he wouldn't do all that bowing," Max said to his sister, as they hurried along the hall. "It's weird."

"Is he the guy who was speaking to Fitz last night?" Kensy whispered, and her brother nodded. "So, did you ask him about Mum and Dad?"

Max shook his head, earning a dig in the ribs from Kensy. No doubt she would have something to say to the man very soon.

CHAPTER 5

ZLKCRPFLK

Kensy's eyes flickered up from her plate toward Song, who, having delivered their meals, was now standing like a sentry by the doorway.

"Is he humming?" she whispered to her brother, who had practically inhaled his breakfast. There wasn't much left on Kensy's plate either.

Max suppressed a smile. He recognized it to be a well-known country and western tune – his sister's least favorite type of music.

"So," Kensy said quietly, "as I was saying

before about the men in the garden . . ." She took her brother's drink and gulped it down, having long ago finished her pineapple juice. Her adventures outside had left her absolutely parched.

Max looked at the emptying glass. "Why are you whispering? And can you stop drinking my apple juice?"

The girl rolled her eyes and plonked the glass on the table. She didn't want Song to hear, in case he was in on the terrible business with the bodies too. "Never mind. I'll tell you later."

Max shrugged and glanced around at the conservatory's white wicker furniture, potted palms and hanging baskets overflowing with red-and-purple fuchsias. "Excuse me, Song, but what does Dame Spencer do exactly?"

"She is a very important businesswoman," Song replied with a smile.

"Isn't a dame like a 'Sir' but for a woman?" Kensy asked.

A bell tinged softly and the butler walked over and opened a cupboard in the wall, producing two plates of hot buttered toast with just the lightest smidge of Vegemite on Kensy's and a lathering of peanut butter for Max. There was hot chocolate too.

"I wonder how Fitz knows her," Kensy said between bites. "I didn't think he knew anyone interesting."

"Apart from us, of course," Max quipped.

Fitz was their father's best friend and, according to family folklore, he'd arrived on their doorstep, heartbroken after his fiancée had called off their engagement. Fitz had remained to help out when the babies were born and had never left, which their mother said was a very good thing given there were no grandparents or siblings on her or Ed's sides of the family. The twins often mused that, for such a lovely guy, who wasn't half-bad looking either, Fitz had a desperately poor track record with the ladies. He kept house while their parents worked, made sure Kensy and Max did their homework and he cooked most of their meals – including a mean apple crumble, for which he'd won several prizes at village fairs on at least three continents. Fitz was also their teacher when school calendars and timetables didn't fit into their movements around the world. The children loved their "manny" as much as their own parents and couldn't imagine life without him, although they were keen for Fitz to find love.

"Max," Kensy said, waving a hand in her brother's face. "Hello . . .? Earth to Max."

The boy, who had been deep in thought, looked up at her with a raised eyebrow.

"Go on," she said, raising an eyebrow to match his. "Ask Song about, you know . . .?"

Max shook his head. "Not yet."

"Why not?" she argued. "You're so stubborn."

"I'm waiting for the right time," the boy said, and chomped into his piece of toast.

Frustrated, Kensy kicked her brother's shin under the table.

"Ow!" the boy yelped. He glowered at her from beneath his hair.

"Fine, if you won't then I will," Kensy huffed, and turned to the butler. "Song, Max heard you say something to Fitz about our parents being missing. What did you mean by that?"

Max cringed inwardly. His sister wasn't the best at playing it cool.

Song's serene expression didn't alter. Kensy may as well have asked for another piece of toast. "Miss Kensington, Confucius says that if what one has to say is not better than silence, then one should keep silent. It is not for me to discuss. You should speak with Mr. Fitz when he returns." He stepped forward and began clearing their plates. "Now, is there anything else I can get for you?"

"What's that supposed to mean?" Kensy demanded.

"Why won't you tell us?" Max asked. He didn't know what he had been expecting from the man, but *that* wasn't it. The boy wondered if butlers observed a code of silence or if Song had been specifically instructed to keep quiet. His right leg began to jiggle up and down as it often did when he was anxious.

Kensy pushed away her plate. "Come on, Max," she said, flinging her napkin onto the table and getting to her feet with such force that the glassware rattled. "I don't know about you, but I've had enough of being kept in the dark."

Max stood up too. "You seem like a really nice person, Song. I wish you'd tell us the truth," he said. Despite the man's unwillingness to share what he so obviously knew, Max had a feeling that Song was the kind of guy you wanted on your team. There was a goodness in his dark eyes. "Please, Song, they're *our parents*. We deserve to know what's going on."

Song nodded and smiled at Max kindly. "Confucius also says three things cannot be hidden: the sun, the moon and the truth. You will have your answer soon enough, Master Maxim."

And with those words of wisdom, a feeling of complete dread clawed at the pit of the boy's very full stomach as he turned to follow his sister.

* * *

"Where are you going now?" Max asked. He could understand why his sister was cross, but he wished she would learn to control her temper. Song definitely wasn't going to tell them anything after that outburst.

"I don't know," Kensy snapped. "I just couldn't stand being in there a minute longer with old Master Confusing. The man speaks in riddles. Why wouldn't he answer the question?"

Max shrugged. "Maybe Fitz told him not to. I can't believe he's gone and left us alone in a strange place with no explanation. It's not like him at all. He could have at least written a note."

Kensy spun around and looked her brother in the eye. Her mouth felt as if it were stuffed full of cotton and her heart was beating madly in her chest. Tears welled in her eyes. "Max . . . do you think it could be true?" she asked in a wobbly voice.

Max reached out and squeezed his sister's hand. "I don't know what to believe, Kens. But until we talk to Fitz, there's no point getting upset. You and I both know how resourceful Mum and Dad are. They save people's lives all the time. They're not about to go and get themselves into trouble."

Kensy hugged her brother fiercely. It didn't happen very often, especially now that they were eleven. As embarrassing as it would be if someone saw them, right at the moment it made them both feel a little better.

"You're right," she whispered. "Why are you always the calm and sensible one?" She fought back another wave of tears and let go of him. "Mum and Dad are fine. They probably just missed a flight or two, that's all." Her eyes lifted to the portraits around the vestibule and she wrinkled her nose at one particularly stern-looking crone. "Do you think she sucked a bag of lemons before she sat for that?"

Max followed her gaze and grinned. "They're all pretty stiff, if you ask me. Although that guy has a friendly face," he said, pointing to a portrait of a man in a military uniform. "He reminds me of someone . . ."

Kensy agreed but couldn't work out who he looked like either. "Let's find out what else is in this palace," she said with a glint in her eye. "We don't know when Fitz will be back, so I think we should start at the top and work our way down and I'll tell you *allllll* about what I heard in the garden. There might be cold-blooded criminals in our midst."

Max stifled a smile. Anyone who knew Kensington Grey was well acquainted with the girl's fanciful theories. "An ax-murdering psychopath, perhaps?"

"You joke now, but you'll see that this time I might just be right," Kensy harrumphed.

The twins bounded up the main staircase, nudging one another as they raced to the top. Max sprinted up two steps at a time and was matched by his sister, who was determined to beat him. They reached the landing and collapsed onto the bare boards, puffing and panting and nearly losing their breakfast.

"I won!" Max declared breathlessly. He stood up and dusted himself off.

"Oh, you did *not*." Kensy rolled away and jumped to her feet. "Right, time to see what's hidden away up here."

The pair walked along the corridor, poking their heads through each and every doorway. As they explored, Kensy told her brother about the vegetable patch and the lady with the squirrel and the conversation she had overheard in the walled garden.

"Should we call the police?" she asked earnestly, once she'd finished. "Or what about MI5 – or is it 6? Aren't they the really cool British spies?"

Max wasn't convinced, but tried to temper his sister's haste tactfully. "Why don't we tell Fitz first?" he suggested. "He'll know what to do."

Kensy nodded. It wasn't the most exciting option, but she reasoned that the murderers might try to do away with them too if they discovered the twins had turned them in to the authorities.

They continued on with Max recounting his morning, including his discovery of *The Caesar Shift* and the encrypted message inside it. Kensy nodded absently and yawned, all the while secretly pleased that her story was way more exciting.

"Do you think she owns a bank or some diamond mines?" Kensy asked.

"Who – Dame Spencer?" Max said. He wondered if Kensy had been listening to him at all – she was clearly thinking about other things. "I suppose she could, but you know some people make their fortunes from really ordinary things. Imagine being the person who invented toothbrushes or sink stoppers."

"Maybe she's one of those rich aristocrats who has inherited their fortune," Kensy mused. "I guess we'll find out eventually. That is, if we're not held here as prisoners for life."

Disappointingly, all the doorways had led to bedrooms. Kensy felt as if she would scream if she saw another canopied four-poster bed or antique side table. After fifteen dead ends, she gave up and slumped onto a burgundy velvet chaise longue at the end of a long corridor.

"Who would've thought that someplace so big could be so boring?" she moaned, pulling a stray leaf from her hair.

"Mmmm," Max replied. He, on the other hand, seemed fascinated by the decor. He was busily running his hands along the papered wall.

Kensy was about to ask what he was up to when a small porcelain dog on the cabinet beside her chair caught her eye. "Hello there," she said, and reached out to pick it up, almost dropping the delicate thing when she was startled by a whirring sound. Kensy turned it over, but there was nothing out of the ordinary. "Max, can you hear this?" she asked, giving it a shake.

"Be careful," Max scolded, when his sister tossed the figurine his way. "This thing is probably worth more than Mum and Dad make in a year."

Kensy curled her feet up on the cushioned seat. "Go ahead and break it then. You never know, we might get someone's attention and possibly even some answers."

Max examined the ceramic creature. He moved it slowly to the left, then to the right, which prompted the same whirring noise as before. His forehead creased with concentration.

"What's the big deal then?" Kensy said impatiently.

"It's a camera," Max whispered, staring into the porcelain pup's eyes.

Kensy looked at him dubiously. "And you give *me* grief about making up wild stories?"

The boy opened the cabinet door and deposited the creature inside.

"Why are you whispering, anyway?" Kensy asked. "Do you think it has a microphone?"

Max shrugged and returned to the wall he had been inspecting.

"What are you looking at now?" Kensy groaned. She glanced around the hallway and wondered if there was anything else spying on them, but there was so much junk it was impossible to tell. Kensy stood up and was alarmed to find her sneakers had left muddy marks on the velvet chaise. Hastily, she covered the evidence with a cushion before her brother could scold her for it, then peered over his shoulder. For the life of her, she couldn't see what had piqued his interest.

"See that there?" Max said, running his finger along an invisible ruler. "That line?"

Kensy squinted at the wall. All she could see were birds and strawberries. "What line?" she grumbled. "This is boring, Max. Can we go downstairs now? There must be a cellar and maybe a secret tunnel or something – anything would be more interesting than *this*."

"Just give me a minute." Max moved on to the cedar table positioned in front of the wall, his fingers skimming the underside of its smooth marble top until they finally found what he'd been looking for all along. "Hey, Kensy," he said, lifting the latch. "Watch this."

"What now, M–?" Kensy's eyes widened as a section of the wall slid back to reveal an alcove with a spiral staircase leading upward. "Whoa. I bet it's the tower at the back of the house. I saw it when I was outside."

Max grinned. "You might be able to pick a lock, sis, but that line in the wall there was a dead giveaway. I knew this was a secret entrance to somewhere," he gloated. He swiftly located the mechanism to close the panel, then turned to ask his sister if she was coming.

But Kensy didn't need an invitation. She was already gone.

CHAPTER 6

QEB QLTBO

Song stared at the portrait, his eyes meeting that of the subject – Cordelia Spencer's long deceased husband, Dominic. He waited until he heard the door click and pushed it open, immediately realizing he was not alone.

"I wondered where you two had gone." He raised his eyebrows and was greeted with a thumping of tails. "So, what do you think of our new arrivals?"

The two dogs simultaneously tilted their heads to the left.

"Yes, I agree Miss Kensington is a feisty one. Both she and her brother are very clever."

Song glanced up at the wall of screens and recoiled. He watched for a few more seconds – long enough to know that his attention was required.

"Perhaps they are too clever for their own good," he added, and quickly left the room.

* * *

"This is so cute," Kensy said, holding up a tiny dress with smocking. She and Max had reached the first floor of the tower to find it filled entirely with children's clothing, from baby onesies to tween apparel. There were racks upon racks, all perfectly organized in ascending order of sizes. "Isn't there a photo of me in a dress just like this when I was about four?"

Max eyed a pair of denim overalls that reminded him of ones he'd owned when he was six. "I do remember something similar, and I had a blue shirt with an awful round collar straight from the nineteenth century."

"You mean like this?" Kensy held up a blue shirt. It had leaves embroidered on the collar.

"*Exactly* like that," Max replied, looking perturbed.

Kensy made a face and placed the item back where she'd found it. "How embarrassing. I don't know what Mum was thinking."

"Some poor kid who lived here must have suffered the same crime against fashion," Max said. "There are enough clothes here to open a shop."

"Or two," his sister agreed. "I'm going to the top. I hope it's not just more of the same up there."

Kensy bounded to the next floor with Max right behind her and the two of them emerged into an identical square room. However, unlike the floor below, where there were no windows, this room was surrounded by sixteen of them. Tall and arched, there were four windows on each side. The racks of clothing had been replaced by mahogany drawers that lined three of the walls and there was a long bench spanning the width of the fourth.

"Well, this is even more boring than the wardrobe," Kensy complained. She climbed onto the bench to see if she could reach the windows, but they were still too high.

Max laughed. "What were you expecting? A torture chamber?"

"No," Kensy said, rolling her eyes. "That would obviously be in the dungeon, which would be located in the cellar, which is exactly where we are heading to next!" She checked the room for any signs of a surveillance camera. "So, are you absolutely sure that dog had a camera in it?"

"I think so. I could break it and know for certain, but Dame Spencer might not be very happy if I did," Max said. He was debating whether or not to snoop around the drawers. It was none of his business, but a part of him wanted to find out more about this strange place.

"She seems to be a bit paranoid about security," Kensy said, jumping to the floor and diving into a drawer of paperwork. "Although it's not that good. I mean, you got us in here without any trouble at all. I wonder what she's trying to hide. Do you think there are more cameras hidden around the house?"

"I'd put money on it," Max said. He decided to take a peek and pulled open the drawer closest to him. It was full to the brim with rolled-up architectural plans. "Anyway, if you were this rich, you'd probably be serious about security too," the boy added.

"True," Kensy said.

Max removed one of the plans and unfurled it on the desktop. He placed a crystal paper-weight on each end to keep it flat.

Kensy walked over to take a look and recognized the front facade. "That's the house," she confirmed with a nod. "It's pretty amazing, isn't it? And let me guess, you saw a mansion just like this one on some boring old show and they kept all the records in a tower."

Max looked up and blinked. "Actually, I think I did," he said, without a hint of irony.

As he rerolled the page and put it away, Kensy opened another drawer. In the front was a bundle of small certificates, the sort kids might get at school. She pulled one out, but before she could take a good look at it, footsteps sounded on the stairs.

"Miss Kensington, Master Maxim," Song's voice echoed from below. He didn't sound angry, but he probably wasn't bringing them ice cream either.

Kensy quickly closed the drawer and managed to shove the certificate into the back pocket of her jeans just as the butler appeared.

"I have been looking for the two of you," Song said.

Kensy arched an eyebrow. "Why? Have you finally decided to tell us the truth about our parents?"

Max shot his sister a warning look.

"What?" she said, firing an equally fierce glare back at him.

Song clasped his hands together and smiled. As much as he would have liked to share his insights, that information was outside the bounds of his authority. It pained him to think of the children's uncertainty, but there was little he could do about it except to keep them occupied until Mr. Fitz returned.

"I am afraid you have stumbled upon the least exciting room in the entire house, which is quite a feat on your part. How about I rectify the situation? Allow me to give you a proper tour of the estate after lunch," he offered. "Now, I hope that you both like lasagna. Mrs. Thornthwaite has prepared her special homemade recipe with salad and teeny tiny crispy potatoes," the man said, pinching the air with his forefinger and thumb. "She is a brilliant cook, even though she has never managed to master the art of dumplings." His voice dropped to a whisper. "Hers are so hard we could use them for ammunition if ever we were under attack. But don't tell her I said so – that woman does not take criticism well at all."

Kensy bit her lip to stop from laughing. But no matter how hard she tried to maintain a sullen face, the corners of her mouth insisted on lifting upward.

Max, however, felt a tug of concern. It seemed weird that, of all the dishes in the world, they would be having their father's favorite meal. First their favorite breakfast and now this? It was certainly suspicious and reminded Max that, without their mum and dad and Fitz, he and Kensy were a long way from home.

Song bowed, motioning for the children to go ahead. He took one last look around the room to ensure nothing had been disturbed before hurrying after them.

CHAPTER 7

JFJ

"*I* thought we would begin with my favorite curiosity in the house," Song said, beckoning them to a dimly lit corner of a small sitting room. "I do not believe in saving the best till last."

The man tugged on a long rope and a light illuminated a glass case. Inside it was a brass elephant, complete with a howdah on its back and surrounded by figurines of men dressed as sultans.

"Are those real diamonds on the wheels?" Max asked, stunned to think that was even possible.

Song nodded. "Isn't it extraordinary? It is an automaton, and was quite popular in the 1800s, but this is one of a kind. There are very few left in the world and none as beautiful as this."

"It's lovely," Kensy admitted. Since she was a toddler, she had loved taking apart machines and putting them back together. She would have liked to do the same to this particular contraption, but something told her Song would be less than impressed. "Why is it tucked away in the dark?"

"Dame Spencer enjoys leaving surprises for her guests," Song replied gleefully. He shuffled around to the other side of the case and pulled a cord protruding from the animal's left hind leg.

The children's eyes were wide with delight as tinkling music filled the air and the elephant began to sway its trunk from left to right, swishing its tail and flapping its leather ears.

Kensy jiggled about excitedly. "Look at those guys – they're supporting Atlas while he's holding up the world, just like the fountain at the front of the house."

Song grinned. "Very observant, Miss Kensington. Now, would you care to see more of the house?" he asked, as a clock on the mantelpiece struck two.

Kensy reluctantly agreed to go as long as she could take a better look at the automaton later on.

Their next stop was a ballroom, followed by a long gallery lined with priceless pieces of art. Max had recognized a couple of paintings, including a Picasso he'd recently completed a project on at school. Impressed by the lad's knowledge, Song showed the children some of the most valuable works in Dame Spencer's collection. Among those of note were wistful countryside scenes by the English painter John Constable, and a painting of a woman and her children by Renoir. Max couldn't help himself and, when no one was looking, traced his finger over the artist's scribbly signature.

Kensy's interest, meanwhile, was visibly waning by the second. "Is there anything else a bit more . . ." She hesitated, trying to think how she could put it politely. Her parents would have been appalled at the way she had spoken to Song earlier; when she reflected on this, her heart hurt and she resolved to do better. "You know . . . exciting?"

Song held up a hand. "Say no more, Miss Kensington. I have a feeling our next destination will be very much to your liking," he said, with a twinkle in his eye.

After yet another wide staircase, Song led the children into a cellar with a curved brick ceiling, but instead of being full of wine bottles, there was a ping-pong table, pinball machines and even a bowling lane with booths and a scoreboard. A huge glass cabinet housed hundreds of board games too. Kensy gasped when she spied a vending machine, which just so happened to be stocked full of the twins' favorite treats. There were even bags of Violet Crumbles, which they'd recently discovered in Australia.

"This is amazing!" Max's eyes darted around the room. "Can we play something?"

Kensy grabbed a paddle and located a couple of ping-pong balls. Her brother hurried to the other end of the table, and the pair engaged in a boisterous set, with Song keeping score. Max narrowly beat his sister by one point, which she hotly contested on the grounds that he had served before she was ready. In protest, Kensy stormed off to play pinball on her own, collecting a snack from the vending machine along the way.

Song took her place and proved to be an outstanding opponent. He soon had Max running from one side of the table to the other without so much as a flick of the wrist. Although Song made a show of patting his brow, Max noticed the butler wasn't puffing at all and hadn't even broken a sweat despite wearing a tuxedo. In the end, Max emerged victorious, though he suspected Song had thrown the last couple of points. Adults did that sometimes and it was really annoying.

Song clapped his hands three times and a twangy guitar immediately began blaring from invisible speakers.

Kensy grimaced. "What *is* that?"

"Isn't it excellent?" Song said, and hummed along to the ditty.

Kensy shook her head. "No, it's horrible," she blurted. Then, remembering she was supposed to be making an effort to improve her manners, added, "It's not really my thing."

"Miss Kensington, you just need to listen for a little while. I guarantee you will not be able to resist the charms of the steel strings," Song insisted.

Kensy arched an eyebrow and grinned. "Just watch me."

Max, on the other hand, happily joined in the humming, much to his sister's disgust.

For the next hour or so, the three of them enjoyed a monumental bowling competition. Max only allowed his mind to wander to his parents once, reminiscing about an evening they'd spent at a bowling alley in Snowmass, Colorado, a couple of years ago. His dad and Fitz were so competitive that the people in the lane next to them seemed genuinely concerned the men were going to end up in a fistfight. But that was just his dad and Fitz. They loved nothing more than a good old contest – a bit like him and Kensy, really.

"I wondered where you lot were hiding," a familiar voice rang out.

Song clapped his hands twice and the music ceased.

"Fitz!" Kensy dropped her bowling ball, narrowly missing her foot, and launched herself at the man's middle. Tears welled in her eyes and, although she didn't want to cry in front of everyone, she was overcome by an avalanche of emotion.

"It's okay, sweetheart," Fitz said, offering the girl his handkerchief. She wiped her eyes and loudly blew her nose.

Max put away Kensy's bowling ball and made his way over, though he hung back slightly further than he normally would have. He didn't quite know how he felt about Fitz right at that moment. "Where have you been?" he asked, unable to keep the hurt out of his voice.

"I'm sorry I left without saying goodbye," Fitz said. He ran his hand over the top of his bald head and took a seat on the edge of an armchair. He looked tired all of a sudden.

"I had a bit of trouble contacting your parents, so I drove down to the embassy . . . to organize a few things."

"What things?" Kensy said, and an uncomfortable silence fell over the room.

"Is it true?" Max asked, staring into Fitz's gray eyes. "About Mum and Dad? Are they really missing?"

The man glanced at Song, then took a deep breath. "Honestly, kids, I don't know. There was a rebel uprising in the area a couple of days ago and the authorities aren't sure what's happened to some of the aid workers." He paused, seeming to search for the right words. "I'll find them, kids, I promise you that. It's quite likely they've sought shelter in one of the local villages and are waiting for the right time to get out. They might need some help making that happen."

Max felt as if he'd been punched in the stomach and Kensy's head was spinning. So their parents might have been kidnapped in Africa and she and Max were as good as kidnapped too, in this strange house with secret cameras and murderers. Kensy blinked back a second wave of tears.

"What do you mean they might need some help?" Max asked. "You're not thinking of going to Africa, are you?"

Fitz nodded.

"Seriously?! Shouldn't you leave the search-and-rescue mission to the experts? It's not like you're a trained commando," Max reasoned.

"What if something happens to you?" Kensy sniffed. "What if you don't come back and they don't either? What will happen to me and Max?"

Fitz was about to reply when an explosion of barking and growling sounded in the hallway outside. Moments later, there was a flash of fur followed by Wellie and Mac in hot pursuit.

The woman Kensy had met earlier in the garden burst into the room, huffing and panting. "You leave Chester alone, you horrible hounds!" she yelled.

But Wellie and Mac were focused on their prey and chased the squirrel across the room. Chester scurried up onto one of the pinball machines, trembling before taking off again, using the furniture to escape his tormentors.

"Wellington, Mackintosh," Song said sternly. His voice was barely above a whisper and yet the two terriers immediately stopped their chasing and settled on the floor by the man's feet. The butler arched an eyebrow at them, prompting the dogs to hang their heads, as if they knew full well they'd just been caught up to no good.

Chester, meanwhile, was now perched on the net of the ping-pong table, twitching tensely and surveying the room. The woman patted her left shoulder and the squirrel took a few running jumps before leaping onto her arm and scampering into the large pocket on the front of her overalls.

Glad of the interruption, Fitz smiled at the woman, who was positively birdlike beside his solid six-foot-four frame. "I see you're still rescuing the wildlife, Mim."

She turned and looked at him for a disconcerting length of time. "Always, darling," she replied, then wrapped her arms around him tightly.

The twins had absolutely no idea what to make of the scene. They'd never heard Fitz talk about anyone called Mim before and here the two of them were carrying on like old friends.

"I don't believe you've met," Fitz said, turning to the children. "Mim, this is Kensy and Max."

Kensy looked at her brother and then back at Fitz. "We sort of did meet, in the garden."

Mim nodded. "I'm sorry I didn't introduce myself properly out there."

Max noticed that her eyes were the most unusual shade of gray just like . . .

"Mim is . . . um . . . she's . . ." Fitz cleared his throat and loosened his collar. He seemed to be blushing, which was very odd indeed, as he was the most unflappable human the twins knew.

"I'm Fitzgerald's mother," Mim said simply. She looked at Fitz, as if to say, "See? That wasn't so hard."

"Fitzgerald?" Kensy repeated. "As in our Fitz?" She turned to him, the question alight in her eyes.

"Well, he's actually *my* Fitz, but I'm happy to share." The woman chortled at her own joke.

For once in her life, Kensy was rendered speechless. Max was also at a loss for words. The two children stood rooted to the spot, processing the fact that the man they thought they knew inside and out had had an entire life before them. It was silly, of course, as well as completely unexpected. If there'd been an electric eel in the bathtub this morning, they couldn't have been more shocked than they were by everything else that had happened today.

CHAPTER 8

ILKALK ZXIIFKD

The Range Rover hurtled along the motorway toward London. The early morning fog had mostly cleared and it was shaping up to be a beautiful day despite Kensy's stormy mood. Fitz was behind the wheel and Song sat beside him in the passenger seat. The butler had swapped his formal attire for more casual clothes, which the children had been glad to see. They hadn't fancied being accompanied around London by a penguin. Wellington and Mackintosh lay between Kensy and Max in the back, sound asleep.

Kensy stared gloomily out the window. She was still hating the fact that Fitz was gallivanting off to Africa and making them attend school in London while he was gone. Apparently, he had some connections there and he thought it the best option, although Kensy didn't really understand it at all. It wasn't fair, and how could she possibly be expected to learn anything when she would spend the whole time worrying about her parents? Her stomach was churning and so was her mind. As the fields flew by, she couldn't help thinking how much their mother would love the lush green countryside. Anna Grey had found Australia rather curious, with the ghost gums and bush. Despite their beauty, she made no secret that she longed for the rolling green hills of her homeland in France.

Song turned on the radio and was soon humming along to the twang of a slide guitar. Kensy groaned and covered her ears while Max, oblivious to the tunes, continued studying the map of London that was spread across his lap. With pointed finger, the boy had followed their journey from North Yorkshire, down the A169 on to the A64 then the M1, which approached the city from the north. He'd been memorizing the names of the towns and villages he could see from the motorway and had just turned the page to focus his attention on the enlarged map of London. They had reached the outer boroughs and were making good time on their run into the city.

Last night the twins had eaten dinner with Fitz and Mim. They still couldn't quite believe that she was his mother, having never heard a word about the woman their entire lives. It transpired that both mother and son were guilty of a family rift and had been equally stubborn about it. But when plans had first gone awry in Zermatt, Fitz had thought the most obvious thing to do was to return home – that way, the children would be in good care if he needed to go looking for Anna and Ed. Sometimes you just had to swallow your pride and, after all, blood was thicker than water.

Max and Kensy had great fun taking turns interrogating Mim for every single embarass-ing childhood story of their stoic manny. They had also learned that Mim managed the gardens at Alexandria and had done so since

Fitz was a boy. The only trouble was, Mim couldn't go down to London with them just now due to some critical work in the garden. She was grafting one hundred experimental new plants – a cross between a blackberry and a raspberry, which they would name a blarsberry if successful. Song had volunteered to accompany them instead, as Dame Spencer was not due back at Alexandria for a couple of weeks and he was happy to assist.

With a captive audience, Kensy had shared what she'd overheard in the garden and announced that they had two criminals, most likely murderers, in their midst – one of whom was going down to London after he'd dealt with some *bodies*.

Mim had thrown her head back and laughed out loud. "Oh dear," she'd said, wiping tears from her eyes. "I'm afraid that some of the staff have an interesting way with words. I do believe that would have been old Shugs, and I understand he and Mr. O'Leary were moving the straw mannequins from the walled field. The local archery club uses them for practice sessions and competitions on the grounds once a month. They would have been sodden from the rain and they weigh a ton when they're wet. Shugs and O'Leary were complaining to me about them yesterday and said that the club should do their own setting up and packing away from now on. Oh, darling girl, I'm so sorry they scared you."

Kensy had felt relieved and disappointed at the same time and a little bit miffed at the smug look on her brother's face. Unfortunately, it all made sense – especially with the arrow in the tree. Just once, though, she wished her nose for trouble was right. Then again, she was glad they didn't have murderers lurking about and that no poor souls had met an untimely demise.

After dinner, the twins had snuck back to the library, where Max had shown his sister the handwritten code in the front of *The Caesar Shift*. Intrigued, Kensy challenged her brother to see who could solve it first. While she tried a few different tacks, giving up on each with an almighty harrumph, Max stuck to one strategy. He used a code Fitz had shown him not long ago. It was called the Caesar cipher, an encryption technique that involved each letter of the alphabet being substituted for another in a fixed pattern. Once Max had discovered that "A" was substituted for "X," he had it transcribed within five minutes. It read:

To our son EDS on the occasion
of your thirteenth birthday.
Welcome to the firm.
With our unwavering love and affection, C & D

It didn't mean anything yet, although Max suspected the "C" stood for Cordelia. They still hadn't gotten to the bottom of what the woman did exactly – besides being a dame, of course. The twins had asked about her over dinner, but it seemed that Fitz and Mim were both experts at deflecting questions they didn't want to answer.

"What's the name of the school we're going to?" Max asked, as he took in the sights and sounds of the city.

"Central London Free School, on Erasmus Street," Fitz replied. "The headmaster is an old friend of mine, and it's close to home."

"Sounds cheap," Kensy grumbled. She ignored the wry smile Fitz flashed her in the rearview mirror.

Max quickly located it on his map. It suddenly occurred to the lad that he didn't know where their new home was. Neither he nor Kensy had thought to ask about their living arrangements until now. There had been too many other thoughts to grapple with. "Where are we staying?" Max asked, but before Fitz could reply, the boy spotted a landmark he knew. "Oh, wow. That's Marble Arch," he declared, putting down the window.

Kensy peered around her brother to see what he was looking at. "How do you even know that?" she muttered.

Max's eyes widened as the car traveled through the roundabout. "And Oxford Street is where you'll find the best shopping in London," he said, gesturing down the road.

"You are correct, Master Maxim," Song said. "I myself am a big fan of Selfridges. Their kitchen department is excellent. They were the only store in the whole city who had a potato peeler in the right shade of crimson."

As the car continued along Park Lane, Max reeled off various other landmarks, including Hyde Park and the Wellington Arch.

"Look!" Kensy pointed excitedly at the cavalry of horses and riders in formation crossing the road ahead of them. She had clearly forgotten to be sullen – for the moment, at least – much to Fitz's relief.

"It's the changing of the guard at Buckingham Palace," Max told her. He glanced at the clock on the dashboard. It was just after eleven in the morning and they'd been traveling since before dawn. "The palace is over there," he said.

"I wonder if Dame Spencer has met the queen," Kensy mused aloud. She began to imagine the two women having sleepovers in their mansions, curling each other's hair and drinking tea while watching silly, old game shows.

"Oh yes, Miss Kensington," Song answered. "They are good friends."

A smile tickled the girl's lips. "Of course they are," she whispered to her brother.

"Mum would love all this," the boy breathed.

Kensy noticed the forlorn look on Max's face and her smile evaporated. "They're going to be okay," she said quietly, then raised her voice for everyone to hear. "I'm not worried, you know. There's no point. Mum and Dad would be cross if they knew we were thinking the worst. Like you said, Fitz, they're probably lying low until that rebel thingy is over."

"You are wise beyond your years, Miss Kensington," Song said with a nod. "Fretting about things that are outside our control is a waste of good energy. It is of far greater use to have a positive attitude."

"Well, I'm not worried either," Max piped up.

Song turned to look at the children in the back seat. "Confucius says you must hold tightly to your hope like a man holds tightly to the rope on a flapping duck's leg in a wild wind."

Fitz and Max burst out laughing. "I bet he didn't," the boy said.

"Yeah, Confucius didn't say that at all," Kensy agreed, catching on. A smile crept back across her face. "You just made that up."

Song pouted. "I am sure if he were here today he would have said it."

And with that admission, the four of them rollicked with laughter. It seemed Song's wise words had an uplifting effect on everyone – Kensy included.

CHAPTER 9

ZBKQOXI ILKALK COBB PZELLI

Kensy leaned against the window and wrinkled her nose. "Is this it?" she asked, as Fitz pulled into the curb. To say she was underwhelmed was putting it lightly.

"Sure is," Fitz replied, hopping out of the Range Rover. He had arranged for Song to take the car and meet them at the town house after their appointment. "Come on, we don't want to keep Magoo waiting."

"Magoo?" Kensy suppressed the urge to say the name again and much, much louder.

"Don't worry – I'm sure there's not a joke

in the world your new headmaster hasn't heard before," Fitz said with a grin. He buzzed the gate and spoke into a small intercom. With a noisy click, they were through to the other side.

"I think this place might actually be a prison," Kensy whispered to her brother. The presence of security cameras, and grilles on all the windows, didn't help to dispel her theory. "Maybe Fitz has gone rogue and he's planning to leave us here."

"I don't think so," Max said, pointing to a small sign. It said CENTRAL LONDON FREE SCHOOL. "Glad it's free, though, because you definitely wouldn't want parents paying for their kids to come here." The squat double-story building had all the character of a brown house brick.

Fitz hit another buzzer and was admitted through a steel-framed door into a reception area. A woman wearing thick black-rimmed glasses and a gray cardigan that looked as if it had been made from a Persian cat sat at a desk in the middle of a small glassed-in room. She had short chestnut hair and long manicured fingernails painted a soft mauve. She stood up and walked to the counter.

"Welcome, welcome," she trilled, her face lighting up the otherwise glum space. "If you could be so kind as to write your names in here," she said, indicating to a ledger, "Mr. MacGregor will be with you shortly."

Fitz entered his name first, then the children's. "Thank you," he said, glancing at the woman's badge, "Mrs. Potts."

The woman smiled and motioned to a row of beige vinyl chairs on the opposite wall. "Please take a seat."

Kensy could feel a piece of torn fabric poking into her leg and began picking at it until Fitz cleared his throat. "I think they need some new furniture," the girl remarked quietly.

She and Max looked around the room. There was a poster about bullying and another advertising a bake sale stuck up on the glass that enclosed Mrs. Potts's office. On the far wall above a set of double doors with glass in the top of them was an honor roll dedicated to the school's head prefects.

One of the doors flew open and a tall lad with wild curly hair thundered through, struggling to balance a huge backpack, a sports bag and a cello case.

"Aren't you forgetting something, Alfie?" Mrs. Potts called after him.

The boy, who was halfway out the door, skidded to a halt and hurried back. "Sorry, Mrs. P. I've got a dentist appointment, and if I miss it I'm a dead man." He scribbled his name in the ledger, then waved with his free hand and ran out the door.

"What a giant," Max gulped. The boy named Alfie looked like he could have done with a shave. "He must be the biggest primary-school kid I've ever seen."

"Oh no, dear, Alfie's in Lower Sixth," Mrs. Potts assured him. "Our school caters for students from juniors right through to A levels."

Max raised his eyebrows at Kensy. This was going to be different.

The headmaster's door opened and a tall, broad-shouldered man in a smart pinstriped suit walked out. He had a pelt of unruly snow-white hair and a tanned complexion, as if he'd just spent a week on a sunny ski slope. Fitz stood up and the two men greeted one another more heartily than the children expected.

The headmaster shook Fitz's hand then slapped him on the back. "It's good to see you, old boy."

"Magoo, how long has it been? Gosh, you're looking fit," Fitz said. "What have you been up to?"

"Spent the summer in the Azores and acquired a perma-tan," the man replied with a grin.

Kensy and Max made faces at each other.

The headmaster turned his attention to the children. "Now, who do we have here?"

"This is Max and his twin sister, Kensy," Fitz said, nodding at them both.

The children stopped gawping and got to their feet, exchanging small hellos and shaking the man's hand one after the other.

"Well, come through and let's have a chat, then we'll have you suited and booted, ready to start tomorrow morning," the burly man said. He led the way into his surprisingly well-decorated office that, oddly enough, wouldn't have looked out of place at Alexandria.

CHAPTER 10

PBZOBQP

"So how do you know Magoo?" Kensy asked, as the children tripped along beside Fitz on the way home.

The man yawned and let out an uncharacteristic sigh. His mind was all over the place and it took him a couple of seconds to realize that Kensy was speaking to him. "Sorry, sweetheart, what did you say?"

"Magoo – how do you know him? It's like you're best buddies," the girl said.

"We went to school together," Fitz replied. "He was always an interesting chap. And it's

Mr. MacGregor to you – get caught calling him Magoo and I suspect you'll be in detention for a month."

"Interesting's one word for him," Max said. The fellow had asked the most random interview questions of any principal the children had ever met. Given the number of schools they'd attended, that was something of a prize. There was none of the regular "What's your favorite subject?" or "What do you like to read?" Instead, Mr. MacGregor had asked Max if he'd ever had the pleasure of swimming with whale sharks, and had inquired after Kensy's preferred choice of winter pudding. The man then went on to share that he was partial to sticky date but only if the butterscotch sauce was piping hot and there was vanilla ice cream to go with it.

True to the headmaster's word, following on from their meeting, the twins had been immediately ushered to a small room just off the school's entrance foyer and, with Mrs. Potts's help, were fully kitted out with uniforms, books and stationery. Strangely, the clothing all fitted perfectly too, which seemed odd considering Kensy always had to have the hems of her dresses adjusted and Max's trousers were never the right length either. It was as if they'd been tailor-made.

"How far is it to the house?" Kensy asked, looking around at the neighborhood. It was a hotchpotch of old and very old buildings. A group of brown-brick buildings took up a block on the left, while opposite – in every sense of the word – was a row of pretty Victorian terraces.

"Not far at all." Fitz glanced at the roadway and headed across. "We're at thirteen Ponsonby Terrace, which is one street after Ponsonby Place. This area is called Millbank and it's just a left, right, then second left from school to home."

A newsagency stood on the corner of a little strip of shops which wrapped around from Ponsonby Place, along John Islip Street to Ponsonby Terrace. Three women huddled together on the sidewalk outside. One was stooped and holding a cane. Her gray hair had a purplish tinge and she looked to be in her late seventies while the other two were younger. Smoke rose from a cigarette the roundest of the three women was holding in her left hand. Her lips bore the wrinkles of a lifetime habit. The third woman had curly brown hair and was dressed in a uniform of an orange shirt and black trousers. They were talking quietly until the woman with the stoop suddenly raised her cane in the air.

"I'm not 'avin' that!" she declared loudly. "It's one in, all in, or else no one's in – that's what I say!"

"Keep your hair on, Esme," the woman wearing the uniform retorted. "And pipe down! Do you want to tell the whole bleedin' neighborhood our business?"

Kensy and Max smiled at each other the way they did when they were sharing the same thought. "Too late – I think she just did," Max whispered.

"Afternoon, ladies," Fitz said as they walked past. He flashed them a good-natured smile.

The three of them looked up at the same time. "Well, 'ello there, lovely," the round woman said. She grinned and raised her eyebrows.

Kensy and Max grimaced at one another.

Fitz and the children weren't more than a few feet past them when the women began to cluck like chickens.

"Gee, Fitz, maybe you actually do have a way with the ladies." Max stifled a laugh before copping a half-hearted elbow to the ribs.

"There's no harm being friendly," Fitz chided. It had been a long time since he'd wandered these streets and he couldn't help thinking that nothing much had changed in the intervening years. There was something comforting about it. His mind ticked over with all the things he had to do. At least he knew Kensy and Max would be in safe hands with Song.

Giggling, Kensy glanced back at the women who had resumed their huddle. She noticed the one with the cigarette pull two envelopes from her pocket and pass one to the lady called Esme and one to the woman in uniform. Wrinkled Lips caught sight of Kensy looking at them and sneered, causing the girl to quickly turn away. Kensy felt a hot flush of guilt – her mother often told her it was bad manners to mind other people's business, but she liked to think of it as being observant rather than nosy. Anyway, those women were up to something. She could sense it.

Fitz and the children turned left into Ponsonby Terrace, where elegant rows of terraced houses were joined together like postage stamps. Some looked to have been converted into apartments, with an entrance at street level and another down a flight of stairs into the basement. Up ahead, Kensy spied the Range Rover parked outside a house with a black door. She wondered if that was where they were staying, although the parking didn't appear to be allocated at all.

Max looked toward the river, which was just on the other side of the busy road at the end of the street. "I know that place across there," he said, jiggling about excitedly. An enormous stone-and-glass building with a curved central facade stood proudly on the opposite side of the Thames. It resembled something a five-year-old might create out of building blocks.

His sister scoffed. "Of course you do, Max. What is it then? The headquarters of some insurance company?"

"For your information, that's MI6," the boy said.

"Really?" Kensy was actually impressed.

Max nodded. "I looked it up after I saw it in a movie. I don't know why you'd tell the whole world the exact location of your national spy organization. Seems quite silly to me."

Fitz suppressed the urge to laugh. "Your brother's right."

Max dusted his knuckles against his chest then blew on them. Kensy just rolled her eyes.

"Here we are – number thirteen." Fitz stopped outside another black door a short distance past the Range Rover. He pulled a set of keys from his trouser pocket and let them inside.

"Whose house is this?" Kensy asked, stepping into a wide entrance foyer. It was elegantly decorated in creams and beiges, with a parquet floor and a huge painting of a stag on the wall ahead. There was something lovely and homely about it, and the air was filled with the delicious smell of baking. Kensy felt a pang of guilt even thinking that – home was with her mum and dad and Fitz and Max, and two out of the five of them weren't there.

"It belongs to Dame Spencer," the man replied.

"Will she be staying too?" Kensy asked, alarmed at the thought. She had concocted such a formidable image of the woman from the bits and pieces of information she had gleaned over the past couple of days that Kensy wasn't sure she ever wanted to meet her.

Fitz shrugged off his jacket and hung it on the end of a row of coat hooks by the front door. "No, she doesn't live here. It's a guesthouse of sorts, for Song or any other staff member who visits London from Alexandria."

"Imagine being so filthy rich that you can have an empty town house in London," Kensy said. "That's mad. And I still can't believe that you have never once mentioned your mother, Fitz. That's a pretty big secret you've been keeping from us. We could have had amazing holidays here and in North Yorkshire, but no, you let a silly argument get in the way of all that."

Fitz grinned. He walked into the sitting room and flipped open a small wooden box on a table beside the sofa, shaking his head as he discovered that, even after all these years, some things never change. "Sorry, Kens. I've had to make some big personal sacrifices to stop the two of you from turning into spoiled brats," the man teased, earning an eye roll from Kensy. "Would you like a chocolate frog?" He didn't wait for the children to answer and threw them two of the foil-covered treats which he'd procured from the box.

"Thanks," the twins chorused, catching their sweets with ease. Max wondered how Fitz knew they were there in the first place.

"Why don't you have a look around?" Fitz said. "There are four floors and your bedrooms are up on the next one. I'll go and see what Song's been up to, but if my nose tells me anything, there should be soup for lunch and cake for afternoon tea and I know I'm starving."

Kensy and her brother charged upstairs, where they located two bedrooms, each with their own bathrooms. One of them was decorated in cornflower blue while the other was white with splashes of red and navy.

"I call the blue room!" Kensy shouted. She ran in and dumped her daypack on the floor.

"You can have it," Max called, walking into the other room. He took in the stylish furnishings and immaculately made bed before turning his attention to the bookshelf, noting some of his favorite titles and a few books he'd been meaning to read.

Kensy padded in after him and picked up a Rubik's cube from the desk. She tossed it in the air absently.

"Don't you think this is a bit weird?" Max said, swiveling around to meet his sister's gaze.

Kensy tilted her head to one side. "What are you talking about?"

"Do you remember the conversation we had with Mum just before she and Dad left for Africa?" the boy said softly. "She asked us what color we'd paint our rooms if we got a choice – which we never do because we're always renting."

Kensy thought for a moment, and her eyes widened. "I said cornflower blue and you said white with touches of red and navy, and I told you that you were always so predictable." She looked around. "I-I'm sure it's just a silly coincidence."

Max opened the wardrobe door, which was full of clothes. They were impeccably ordered with long trousers at one end, shirts and T-shirts in the middle and coats last of all. There were brand-new shoes tucked into their own special pigeonholes. Max pulled out a pair of jeans – the exact ones he'd been begging his mum for and which she'd told him were too expensive. He looked at the size.

"You think this is just a coincidence too then?" he said, holding up the hanger.

"Of course it is. Otherwise that would mean Fitz had planned all this . . ." Kensy stepped forward and riffled through the rest of the clothes, noting that the colors and styles were exactly the sorts of things her brother loved. Then she raced into the other bedroom. Her wardrobe was bursting with clothes in her size and to her taste too, although there was one particularly ugly Christmas sweater with a reindeer and glowing red nose that no one could pay her to wear.

Max followed her and leaned against the door frame. "Well?"

"It's as if they've have been waiting for us," she said quietly. "Why would there be bedrooms in a house owned by some lady we've never met that are set up just for us?"

Max swallowed hard. "I don't know."

Kensy felt a tickle in her nose and sneezed loudly. She reached into the back pocket of her jeans for a tissue and a small square piece of cardboard fluttered to the floor. She knelt down to pick it up.

"What's that?" Max asked.

"It was from one of the drawers in the tower at Alexandria. I put it in my pocket when Song caught us," she said guiltily. "I didn't mean to keep it, but I forgot. I didn't even look at it."

Max took it from her and together they read the contents of the certificate from Jindabyne Central School.

Maxim Grey, for outstanding
work in mathematics

"Why would this have been at the house?" Max asked. "Did you see what else was in that drawer?"

Kensy shrugged. "Maybe Fitz bundled up our things and sent them to the house to be stored. It's not as if they don't have the room and, let's face it, we move all the time."

"Look at the date," Max said. "I only received this the day before we left. The original is still in my bag. I was going to show Mum and Dad when we saw them . . . Why would Fitz send copies of our certificates to Alexandria?"

Kensy's mind was racing so fast she was beginning to feel dizzy. "Come on," she said, snatching back the piece of cardboard, "let's go and see what he has to say about this."

"Wait." Max grabbed her arm. "Think about it, Kens. Fitz never told us about his mother and we don't know much at all about Dame Spencer. We woke up in a mansion in England that we've never heard anything about and now we're here in London in these bedrooms with clothes and things just for us. I don't think we can trust anyone – at least not until Mum and Dad come back."

"Not even Fitz?" Kensy bit her lip. "What if Mum and Dad don't come back?"

Max looked at her. "We can't think like that. We promised."

His sister nodded. "It's so hard. I try not to imagine the worst, but then my brain goes into overdrive and I think: what if they've been captured? Or they're being held for ransom? There are *pirates* off the coast of Africa, Max."

Kensy looked around at the perfect room. Like her brother's, the bookshelves were full of stories she loved and some she hadn't yet read. Even the cushions in the middle of her queen-sized bed reminded her of some she and her mother had recently admired in a catalog. Kensy's eyes fell upon a notepad on the bedside table. She walked over to take a closer look, her heart skipping a beat when she realized the motif was of characters from a book she had long adored. The words below them formed a phrase she and her mother often said to one another, especially when Kensy wasn't quite feeling herself.

"Look," she said, tears welling in her eyes. She tore off the page and showed it to her brother.

"How much do I love you?" Max read aloud.

"To the sun and stars and back again," Kensy recited from memory. Hope swelled in her chest. "It's a sign from Mum. I'm sure of it." She ran to the window, pushing it up then leaning out to look up and down the street.

"Stop and listen to yourself, Kens. It doesn't make any sense," Max reasoned. Now was not the time for one of his sister's flights of fancy.

Kensy turned back to face him. "No, but neither does that merit certificate nor the way Fitz has been acting or anything much that's happened in the past thirty-six hours," she insisted, a determined look in her eyes.

"Kids, lunch is ready," Fitz called up the stairs.

"I think we should find out some more about Dame Spencer," Max said, quickly shutting the window. "But let's keep this to ourselves for the time being, okay?"

Kensy nodded and stuffed the note into her jeans pocket.

"You two okay?" Fitz said, appearing at the door. He glanced from one twin to the other.

"Yes," they answered in unison, earning a quizzical look from their manny.

Max suddenly saw that the certificate was sitting on Kensy's desk in plain view. He dove toward it and pushed it under a decorative box. "Thought I saw a cockroach," the boy mumbled.

"Really? I can get some spray," Fitz said.

"It's okay," Max said. "We lived in Australia – nothing in England could be as bad as some of the bugs there."

Fitz grinned in reply, though he hadn't missed a thing and wondered what the boy had been so desperate to hide from him. He made a note to check under the box later. "So do you like your rooms?" he asked.

"They couldn't be more . . . perfect," Max said, flashing him a smile.

"Oh . . . good," Fitz said, smiling back. "I can't take any of the credit. Song arranged everything. I know he went to great pains to get some clothes and knickknacks he thought you might like."

Kensy shared a look with Max. "Song did all this?"

Fitz nodded. "He's a man of many talents and looking after guests is his specialty. Speaking of which, Song has made us a delicious batch of soup. It's –"

"Let me guess," Max jumped in. "Pumpkin?"

"With a hint of ginger?" Kensy added. She folded her arms across her chest.

"Uh . . . yes." Fitz frowned. "How did you know?"

"Oh, just a guess," Kensy replied, and followed Max out of the room.

Either Song was a mind reader or there was something much stranger going on.

CHAPTER 11

CFOPQ AXV XDXFK

"*Song* doesn't have to come and get us this afternoon," Max said. He turned to Fitz, who was walking behind him and Kensy. "We're more than capable of making our own way home. We're eleven, not seven."

"We'll see about that," Fitz said. Although he knew the lad was right, he wasn't prepared to take any risks. There was too much at stake.

"What time are you leaving?" Kensy asked. She clutched the piece of notepaper she'd put into the pocket of her uniform.

"As soon as you two are safely deposited

at school," Fitz replied. "But it will take me a couple of days to get there, so don't expect to hear anything right away."

Max looked over at his sister, half expecting her to spill the beans on what they'd found yesterday. He was impressed she'd kept it to herself for so long, considering they'd spent the late afternoon with Fitz seeing some sights around the city. They'd driven past Buckingham Palace and Trafalgar Square and taken a spin on the London Eye. While it was exciting to see London, both children found themselves thinking how much more fun it would be if their parents were there too.

As they neared the school, Kensy slowed to a crawl. "Um, Fitz?" she said in the coy manner she used for getting her own way. "We're going to miss you lots, but you really don't need to walk us all the way to the gates."

Fitz stopped on the sidewalk in surprise, then noticed the girl looking shyly around at the students milling past them. "What? You don't want me to lick my fingers and clean your faces at the gates?" he teased.

Kensy wrinkled her nose. "Ew! I remember when you did that to me outside my nursery school in Banff. That horrible boy . . . I can't remember his name . . ."

"Jacob," Max said, without glancing up from his Rubik's cube. He'd already solved it twenty-six times that morning but was eager to beat his fastest time of two minutes and ten seconds.

"That's right. After he saw you do it once, he would lick his fingers and try to wipe them on me whenever he thought he might get away with it," Kensy said, shuddering at the memory.

"All right," Fitz relented. "Have a good day. Song *will* be here this afternoon. Just for today, I promise," he said, when he spotted Kensy's scowl. "I'm sure you'll be fine to walk on your own tomorrow." He smiled, but there was a tightness in his face. "So I don't suppose you want a hug then?"

Avoiding his sister's gaze, Max went in for a squeeze. He wouldn't admit it to anyone – least of all himself – but he was afraid that he might never see Fitz again.

"Try to enjoy it, mate," Fitz said, ruffling the boy's hair. "And no worrying, Kensy."

"Be safe," she said, giving him a quick hug too.

With a wink and a wave goodbye, Fitz turned to leave. Max took off toward the school gates and was almost there when he realized Kensy wasn't beside him. She was still standing where Fitz had left them, staring across the street.

Kensy watched as a round woman with a cigarette trailing smoke from her left hand passed an envelope each to two ladies. It was the same trio they'd seen outside the newsagency the afternoon before, but this morning they were standing in the forecourt of the red-brick apartment building across from the school.

"I see Fitz's girlfriends are at it again," Kensy mumbled to herself.

The woman with the walking stick was wearing a thick tartan coat and had a scarf on her head. Kensy caught a glimpse of the rollers underneath and grinned. This time they weren't squabbling – just shivering, by the looks of them. She wondered what was in the envelopes. Bingo winnings or maybe they liked to exchange recipes. The girl's imagination was off and racing when her brother's voice interrupted her thoughts.

"Come on, Kensy, we'll be late," Max said, running back to fetch her.

"And that's the last thing you'd want to be on your first day," said a clipped voice from behind them.

The twins turned to see a tall, thin woman with a tangle of dark, curly hair.

"Romilly Vanden Boom, science," she barked by way of introduction. "Now, if I were you two, I'd get a move on. Mr. MacGregor's a stickler for punctuality, and you have an assembly to get to."

She charged through the surge of students, who all seemed to be arriving at exactly the same time.

The twins were swept in through the front doors of reception, where Mrs. Potts gave them a grin and a wave despite the dozen students competing for her attention.

"Gee, she's lovely," Kensy said. "I think she actually smiles sunshine."

Max grunted in reply. His eyes were all over the place, taking everything in as they were carried to their lockers on the tide of students. Kensy stopped in front of hers while Max continued further down to his.

Kensy was wrestling with her padlock when she suddenly felt a sharp dig in her left rib cage. "Ow!" she yelped, and spun around, intending to give the culprit a good talking-to.

A girl with long dark hair piled on top of her head closed her locker door. "Newbie alert," she sang to the girl beside her, who giggled. They looked older than Kensy, although perhaps it was just the full faces of makeup they had on. The dark-haired girl turned to Kensy and raised a perfectly plucked eyebrow. "So who are you?"

Forgetting herself, Kensy squeaked her full name.

"Really?" The girl smiled, but it wasn't a sweet one like Mrs. Potts's. "Your name's Kensington? That's so funny because mine's Mayfair and hers is Knightsbridge. Apparently, everyone at this school is named after a posh part of London."

"Oh, stop it, Lola," a tiny voice chirped. "There's really no need for you to give every single person who starts at this school a hard time, is there? And you can zip it too, Misha."

Lola narrowed her ice-blue eyes at the girl. "Can't you take a joke, Autumn? Then again, you'd know exactly what it's like to have a ridiculous name. Thank goodness my mother called me something sensible."

"Are you joking? Your surname is Lemmler." Autumn rolled her eyes. "Try saying that ten times without tripping over your tongue."

Lola's eyes narrowed. "You're so mean!" she spat, then looped her arm through Misha's and flicked her bangs back across her eyes before the pair sloped off down the hall.

The smaller girl turned to Kensy. "Ignore those two. Lola hates new kids as a rule, especially if they're smarter or prettier than her, and Misha's never had an original thought in her life. As you probably heard, I'm Autumn, and I assume you're Kensington. It's good to meet you."

"Hi. Kensy's fine," the girl said, hugging her books to her chest. She wasn't used to anyone defending her like that, except for Max on the odd occasion. It was usually up to Kensy to deal with the mean kids and, having lived all over the world, experience taught her there was one or two in every school. It was kind of nice not having to be the tough one for a change. She smiled at the girl. "Thanks for that, by the way. And don't worry, I promise I can give as good as I get."

Autumn was quite a bit shorter than Kensy and was what her mother would have described as immaculate. Her glossy black hair was pulled into a low ponytail and tied with a red satin ribbon the same shade as their school sweater. Her fingernails were filed into neat crescent moons and her skin was like caramel milk. She wore smart red-rimmed spectacles and was carrying a small pile of books.

Further down the hallway, Max had completely missed the drama, having enjoyed a civilized conversation with a lad called Carlos. The pair walked over and introduced themselves and, before they knew it, another five kids had joined their huddle.

Autumn pointed at each of them. "This is Harper, Dante, Inez, Yasmina and Sachin. Our new friends are Kensington and Maxim, but they prefer Kensy and Max."

There was a laugh followed by a swift round of hellos.

Kensy liked the way Autumn introduced her and Max as their new friends, as if it were a foregone conclusion. She was silently repeating their names in her head and memorizing things about them. Harper was blonde with the palest blue eyes; her hair fell in loose ringlets framing her heart-shaped face. Dante was tall and dark with chestnut hair. Inez had a smattering of freckles across her nose and a sweep of long copper curls. Yasmina's chocolate eyes were almond-shaped and she had an aquiline nose and a navy headscarf, and Sachin was olive-skinned with black hair and eyelashes to die for.

"We'd better get to the hall or Magoo will make a spectacle of us all," Autumn said, eyeing her watch.

"You don't really think he'd get the canons out again, do you?" Dante said with a pained expression.

Kensy blinked in alarm. "Canons! You're joking, right?"

"Have you met our headmaster?" Sachin grinned. "He's as mad as a hatter. Just wait until you see what he gets up to."

Harper shrugged. "At least school is never dull."

Kensy and Max looked at one another. It sounded as if Central London Free School was going to be far more interesting than they'd first imagined.

CHAPTER 12

X ZEXIIBKDB

Kensy and Max found themselves in the middle of the front row of the hall between their new friends. Despite the promise of a spectacle, they were lulled into a glassy-eyed state by a litany of announcements. A teacher dressed in a red-and-navy tracksuit talked about an upcoming competition. Autumn whispered to Kensy that his name was Mr. Nutting and he was an Olympic archer. Following on were notices about debating, a fundraiser and auditions for a play before Mr. MacGregor took to the podium.

He regaled the assembly with a blow-by-blow account of his golf game the previous weekend, including reenactments of his swing and stumbling down an embankment, which had everyone guessing as to what point he was trying to make – or whether he just really liked talking about golf. After what seemed a very long time, he did relate the game back to the idea of challenging oneself against any perceived handicaps. His joyous mood turned decidedly dark thereafter as he disintegrated into a rant about laziness and lack of direction.

"Not this again," Autumn groaned, as two exercise bikes were wheeled onto the stage by the custodian. They were curiously facing away from the audience. When Kensy asked her what it all meant, the girl grimaced. "You'll see."

"Do I have a volunteer?" the headmaster boomed.

Nobody moved. Hands were firmly clasped in laps and eyes focused straight ahead.

Kensy wondered what was wrong with them all – surely whatever the headmaster was proposing couldn't be that bad. She was about to raise her hand when she felt a sharp nudge from Autumn and decided against it. Max, meanwhile, had taken a sudden interest in his shoes.

Carlos looked over at him and blanched. "Oh no, you don't want to look down otherwise –"

Too late.

"Maxim Grey!" the headmaster exclaimed. "Brand-new today and he's already volunteered. Please make your way to the stage – there's a fine lad."

Max froze. "But, I . . . I didn't volunteer, sir."

"Of course you did! The minute you looked away, you were mine." The man waggled his eyebrows somewhat maniacally.

"What's going to happen?" Kensy whispered, as Max made his way to the stage. In the row behind them, Lola snickered loudly, adding to Kensy's mounting unease.

Max glanced back at the crowd and almost wished he hadn't. They looked like a pack of grinning hyenas. Kensy touched her left earlobe, and Max flashed a tense smile then did the same. It was their secret signal that everything was going to be all right – they hoped.

The headmaster pointed to one of the stationary bikes. "Hop up there, son. You and I are going to have a race."

Max recoiled. "A race, sir? You and me?"

"Yes, of course you and me. Just because I'm over the age of eighteen doesn't mean I'm past my sell-by date!" Magoo rolled his eyes at his staff, who giggled like schoolgirls.

Max climbed onto the seat, and the custodian set about making adjustments. He also equipped both the headmaster and Max with small microphones pinned to their shirt collars. Magoo, it seemed, liked to commentate the event, although it was a little risky having the student on a mike, given one past episode when his opponent completely forgot himself and swore loudly no less than three times.

"He's a dead man walking," Sachin murmured. "Or should I say sitting? Magoo never loses. He knows London like the back of his hand."

All eyes watched as a giant screen descended from the ceiling. The teachers who had been sitting across the stage stood up and moved their chairs off to the sides.

"What's the challenge this time, sir?" a lad called out.

"Let's see," Magoo said, tapping his chin. "Mr. Reffell, our esteemed history teacher, can nominate the destination."

A teacher dressed in a black academic gown stood up and walked to the podium while the headmaster quickly briefed Max on the rules of the activity.

"Does this happen very often?" Kensy asked. She noticed that the screen directly in front of the stationary bikes now displayed the view of the street outside the school gates. Judging by the traffic whizzing to and fro, and the time stamp in the corner, it appeared to be streaming live.

"About once a term. It's actually hilarious, unless you're the poor kid up there," Autumn said. "But your brother looks pretty calm for someone who's about to be completely and utterly humiliated in front of the entire student body."

Kensy grinned with an air of confidence Autumn feared was extremely misplaced. "Don't be so sure of that. My Max can . . . well, let's just see what happens."

"I think, Mr. MacGregor, that your destination will be Westminster Cathedral," Mr. Reffell announced.

The headmaster nodded. "Good choice, old chap. I'll be there in a jiffy."

"Excuse me, sir, but can I ask how this thing works?" Max fiddled with the handlebars on the bike. "If I turn a particular way, will I go there on the map or the street view?"

"Aha! Very good question, dear boy. The answer is yes to both, but you can't see the maps, can you? They are behind us, so unless you have eyes in the back of your head, I assume the answer is no."

Magoo removed his blazer and threw a yellow bicycle helmet to the boy before plonking a blue one onto his own tuft of snow-white hair.

"The screen will split in two," he continued, "so you can see where you're going and I'll see where I'm going. Unless, of course, you'd prefer to eat my dust the whole way?" The headmaster chortled, stretching his hamstrings.

Max gripped the handlebars and swiveled them about, realizing that on the screen he'd turned to face the other way. He quickly pedaled back into position.

"Ready?" Magoo looked over at the boy, who sucked in an anxious breath.

Max nodded. "May I ask what the prize is, sir?"

"Good heavens above, I think Maxim actually believes he might beat me!" Magoo looked at his staff, some of whom were slapping their knees and guffawing.

"I don't think I will, sir. I know it," Max muttered under his breath, forgetting for a second that he was on a mike. His words hissed out from the speakers, garnering a loud gulp from the assembly.

Carlos shook his head sadly. "He's really going to cop it now. He'll be on Kevin duty for the rest of the term."

Kensy was almost afraid to ask. "Who *is* Kevin?"

"Magoo's Venus flytrap," Carlos explained. "Whoever has to look after Kevin –"

The boy's words were drowned out by a loud thumping beat as "The Eye of the Tiger,"

116

one of Fitz's favorite training songs, blared from the speakers.

"Ready?" the headmaster shouted. "On your mark, get set, go!"

Magoo began pumping the pedals, leaving Max sitting outside the school gates. But the lad was determined and in his mind's eye he was looking at the map of London he'd committed to memory. He sprinted into action, following the headmaster down Erasmus Street. He then peeled off, veering left into a side road and garnering a collective groan from the assembly.

"He's done for. That's a one-way street," Carlos murmured. "It's against the rules."

Lola sniggered loudly, earning a glare from Kensy.

Max soon recognized his mistake and did a U-turn, emerging back on to Erasmus Street. By now, the headmaster was ahead by two hundred yards. When the boy turned left on to Page Street, Magoo grinned like a Cheshire cat. Maxim Grey clearly had no idea where he was going. Perhaps he'd been a little unkind in choosing the lad, but it would be a good test nonetheless. The headmaster was about to turn right into Horseferry Road when a kid bellowed, "Mr. Reffell said Westminster Cathedral, not the Abbey!"

Magoo hit the brakes so hard he almost flew over the handlebars. "No! No, no, no!" he yelled, furious with himself for being so careless. He quickly backtracked and sped along Horseferry Road, which for a little way ran parallel to the street Max was on.

The boy, meanwhile, was sure there'd be a tiny alley up ahead that would provide a shortcut.

"No! It's a dead end!" a girl called.

But Max trusted his instincts. It was a good thing too because he was right. He pedaled harder, as if his life depended on it – which, at the moment, he thought might actually be the case.

Perspiration was now pouring from the headmaster's brow as he rounded the corner into Greencoat Place. He let out an astonished cry as he spied Max flash past on a street up ahead. "Heavens to Murgatroyd, how did you get there?" he yelled, and stood up on his pedals, pumping his legs faster and faster.

The students leaned forward in their seats and watched as the blue and red dots converged upon Westminster Cathedral.

"Look out!" Kensy screamed as her brother swerved to miss a London bus that had turned a corner sharply into his path.

It felt as if the hall roof was about to lift off with all the cheering and stamping and shouting.

"Go, Max!" Kensy leapt to her feet and was joined by the rest of the children. Except for Lola and Misha, who were sitting with their arms folded in sullen protest. Kensy jumped up and down screaming as her brother pedaled furiously. He took another turn away from the main road, which was met with more groans but proved once again to be right.

Magoo was struggling to retain any composure at all. "Nooooo!" he puffed, barely able to get the word out.

Max turned the final corner and swerved in and out of oncoming traffic before dodging a lady with a baby in a pram and executing a skid against the cathedral steps, which was no mean feat on a stationary bicycle.

The assembly went wild.

"You're a legend, Max!" one lad yelled.

"You're my hero!" a girl exclaimed. "Do you have a girlfriend?"

Max turned bright red and was glad he was facing away from the crowd.

"He's eleven!" Kensy scolded.

The girl, who looked to be at least fifteen, winked at Kensy. "He's not my type, anyway."

"That's good because I think he could be mine," Autumn breathed, then glanced around, hoping no one had heard her.

Max jumped off the bike, removed his helmet and ran his fingers through his hair, restoring it to perfection. He walked over to shake hands with Mr. MacGregor, who had finally reached the destination. The headmaster almost fell off his bike, his trembling legs barely able to hold his own weight.

Daphne Potts appeared from the side of the stage carrying a tray with two large glasses of ice water. She quickly passed one to her boss and one to Max. A hush fell over the assembly as the lad held out his hand.

"Do you think he'll get into trouble for winning?" Kensy whispered to Autumn.

"Who knows what Magoo might do – no one's ever beaten him at a cycling race before," the girl gushed, unable to tear her eyes from the winner. "This is totally outside my experience."

"First day here, Maxim Grey, and you've managed to defeat me. I think that deserves –" there was a pregnant pause and the entire school swallowed in unison – "a handshake," the headmaster said with a grin. The students clapped and stamped their feet. Magoo leaned in close to Max, removing his lapel mike and covering Max's with his other hand. "How did you do it?" he asked.

"I just have this thing, sir, where I can look at a map and remember it," Max said. "All of it."

The man patted the lad on the back. "Well, Maxim, that's a wonderful skill to have. Good for you."

Afterward, the children spilled out of the school hall, all a-chatter. The only name on anyone's lips was Maxim Grey. So it seemed, whether the boy liked it or not, he had just acquired something akin to hero status.

CHAPTER 13

PZFBKZB IBPPLK

As the children romped along the corridor to their first class, Max collected a steady stream of high fives and pats on the back. He'd certainly won the admiration of his peers and, while Kensy was rightly proud of her brother, she couldn't help feeling a twinge of jealousy too. They'd been at school less than an hour and everyone knew Max's name.

Autumn led the way into a bright-white room. Kensy's jaw dropped as she cast her eyes about. Unlike their primary school science classes, which were generally conducted in the ordinary classroom or at best in a room with a few bits and pieces of scientific-looking equipment, this was a proper lab. There were gas burners on the benches as well as an array of beakers and tubes. Kensy marveled at a distillation process taking place at the front of the room, only to turn and find a collection of deceased creatures, perfectly preserved in tall jars of formalin. To top it off, there was a large glass tank with a piece of driftwood, and coiled around it was a pretty yellow snake.

Max walked over to take a closer look.

"That's Beatrice," Carlos said, as the serpent's tongue flicked in and out. "She's a corn snake. Those guys over there are her dinner."

Max glanced across the room at a cage wriggling with little brown mice. "Really?"

"No, just kidding," Carlos said, grinning. "We feed Beatrice dead rats that Mrs. Vanden Boom says she gets from the sewers. We think she's joking too, about where she gets them — although you know London is crawling with rodents. She'd be doing the city a favor."

Max grimaced. He hoped he wasn't given snake-feeding duties. The idea didn't sound remotely appealing no matter what they fed the creature.

Along with Beatrice and the mice, there was a giant stick insect called Mr. Badger – apparently because of an unusual stripe on the creature's head. Max couldn't even see it, camouflaged as it was in a glass case full of foliage.

Mrs. Vanden Boom walked briskly into the room dressed in a white lab coat with her name embroidered on the breast pocket. She gave a brief welcome, then ordered them all into their seats and made mention of their two new classmates.

The room was laid out three benches deep and two across, each catering for four or five students. Kensy and Autumn slid onto two stools beside Max and Carlos.

Romilly Vanden Boom turned to Max. "That was an extraordinary display in assembly, young man. Now, I think your sister deserves an opportunity to shine as well." The woman raised her eyebrows at Kensy, who gulped, wondering what the teacher had in mind. "This morning we're going to build a robot using motors from various household appliances. Is that something that would interest you, Kensington?"

Kensy couldn't believe her luck. She loved nothing more than pulling things apart and putting them back together again and had recently been in a huge amount of trouble for dismantling the blender at home. But the look on her mother's face when she had reassembled it with an extra top speed option was priceless. Kensy felt a burst of happiness followed sharply by an overwhelming sadness. She couldn't wait to see that look again.

Max nudged his sister. "She's talking to you."

"Sorry," the girl said, recovering quickly. "I was just thinking about . . . how much I'd enjoy it."

"Wonderful," Mrs. Vanden Boom said, looking pleased. "Why don't you pop up here and help me pull apart this motor? It's from Mr. MacGregor's coffee machine, but I won't tell if you don't." The woman gave a sly wink. "I'm sure we'll have it returned to him spick-and-span before he has time to miss it."

Kensy smiled. "If you say so."

* * *

Magoo MacGregor walked into his office from the en suite bathroom that was accessed via a hidden door behind a bookshelf. He couldn't stand the thought of having to share the staff bathroom, particularly as he rode to work no matter the weather, and so had it put in years ago. He pushed the shelf back against the wall just as Daphne Potts entered with a tea tray.

"I don't imagine you were expecting that, sir." She placed the tray on the edge of his vast desk and proceeded to pour a cup from the teapot.

"No, especially since the lad's never set foot in London before. Apparently, he has a photo-graphic memory – for maps, at least. That will no doubt serve him well," the headmaster said, and sat down in his black leather armchair. "I suspect he's been elevated to hero status with the students, so he can thank me later. Anything urgent I should know about for today?"

Mrs. Potts pulled a small notepad from her trouser pocket and read down the list. "No, no, my problem. No. Oh! Monty Reffell would like to squeeze in a chat about the upcoming history tour to Rome. He wants to check that everything's in order." Mrs. Potts continued scanning the items on her list. "No, no, no, I can fix that. Oh, yes. Romilly asked to see you downstairs. She says she's finished that new watch for you."

"Ooh, goody! And does it have the . . .?" Magoo jiggled his eyebrows, setting his teacup down with a chink.

Daphne Potts nodded.

"Oh, I knew she could do it." The headmaster grinned like a boy who had just realized it was Christmas tomorrow. "The woman's a genius. Buzz Eric, will you? Ask him to meet me there at eleven hundred. He'll get such a kick out of it."

"Very good." Mrs. Potts flicked her notepad shut and headed for the door, then stopped and turned back. "How long do you think we'll have the twins, sir?"

Magoo rested his chin in his hand. "Fitz is hoping all will be resolved in a couple of weeks. I'm afraid I don't share his confidence."

Daphne bit her lip. "How much do they know?"

"Nothing, so we keep things shtum for now."

"Of course, sir." Mrs. Potts left the room and closed the door behind her. It broke the woman's heart to think of what those poor children were going through and it was likely just the beginning. Eleven years old and they didn't even know who their parents really were.

CHAPTER 14

PRPMFZFLK

Kensy glanced at her watch. She could hardly believe it was almost three o'clock. School had never gone this quickly before – except for Wednesdays last term, back in Australia, when they would head to Thredbo for sports. Having grown up on ski slopes around the world, though, downhill race training was mostly just fun for the twins.

After science, they'd had mathematics. Their teacher, a tiny waif of a woman called Miss Ziegler, zipped about the classroom like a flea in a bottle, checking that everyone knew exactly what she was talking about.

Kensy loved math and had no trouble with any of it. At the start of the lesson, Miss Ziegler had pointed to a puzzle on the board. There was a buzz around the room as the kids all offered their opinion on who would be the first to solve it. The hot tip was a rakish boy named Graham, but he seemed to spend a lot of time scratching his head, which made Kensy wonder if he might have nits – which then caused her to spend an inordinate amount of time scratching her own head. Kensy thought she was just about to solve it when Max stood up and walked to the front of the room to write his answer. There was a groan as the children realized he was right. He was rewarded with a bag of red frogs that his sister Kensy made sure he shared with her and their new friends at lunchtime.

Their history lesson was interesting, to say the least. Mr. Reffell entered the classroom dressed in full colonial costume and assumed the character of Admiral Horatio Nelson. Kensy had never even heard of the man, but by the end of the lesson there wasn't much she didn't know about the Battle of Trafalgar and the defeat of "that upstart Frenchman Napoleon Bonaparte." She'd held her breath when Mr. Reffell had drawn a very large sword and lunged at one of the boys, the tip connecting with the flushed skin on the lad's neck.

Kensy had been thrilled to find out they were studying French as both she and Max were fluent speakers. Their teacher, Madame Cosette Verte, had the most welcoming smile and her long brown hair swished about her shoulders as she spoke. She wore a dress covered in pink flowers with matching lipstick and Kensy soon decided she was one of those people who simply radiated joy. Madame Verte had beamed at Kensy and Max when they initiated a conversation in French that she joined in with great enthusiasm.

The twins' English teacher, on the other hand, was a bit snippy. Although her name made Kensy think of someone round and squishy, she was all bones and angles. Miss Witherbee was tall and had the sort of frame fashion designers preferred to dress, like a walking coat hanger. It quickly became evident that the woman had no patience for anyone in the class who didn't "get it" straightaway. Then again, Kensy couldn't stand it when teachers had to go over and over things either, so she felt the woman's pain when a pallid boy called Winston made her explain their homework at least three times. Kensy noticed a little vein pop out on the side of Miss Witherbee's temple each time the lad said, "But I still don't get it."

While Kensy and Max remained together for all of their lessons, Autumn and Carlos and the rest of their new friends attended advanced classes for a couple of periods. Kensy was nothing but determined that she and Max would join them soon.

Their friends had met them in the dining hall for lunch, and enjoyed a meal of roast chicken, vegetables and gravy. It was different to school in Australia, where they'd usually taken a packed lunch from home. The head dinner lady, Mrs. Trimm, had given Kensy an extra serving of sticky date pudding with butterscotch sauce and vanilla ice cream, which was delicious. Kensy had watched

Mr. MacGregor devour his. It was comforting to know that Mrs. Trimm's cooking met his exacting standards.

The last lesson of the day was PE and involved a vigorous game on a field at the back of the school. Max scored two goals, well and truly cementing his legendary status. But it was Kensy who booted three balls into the back of the net, and was beginning to accumulate her own legion of fans – but only from their class.

Their teacher, Mr. Nutting, let the kids get changed and go to their lockers before the bell. Kensy was just working out what she needed to take home when Max tapped her on the shoulder.

"I'll meet you at the front gates," he said. He was still being high-fived and patted on the back by just about every student, which Kensy was starting to find quite irritating.

Luckily, Autumn appeared at the locker beside her, lifting her mood.

"Hey," Kensy said brightly, "what lesson did you come from?"

Autumn glanced at her and smiled. "PE," she said, rolling her eyes. "My worst subject."

"That's funny," Kensy said. "I didn't see you out there."

"Oh no, I'm in a different class than you. We were doing theory today – um, resuscitation," Autumn replied, hurriedly shoving books in her bag. She zipped it closed and shut her locker door. "I'll see you tomorrow."

"Oh, okay. I thought you might like to . . ." Kensy stopped, realizing the girl was jiggling about as if desperate to rush off. She had been planning to invite Autumn over after school, but perhaps it was better if she asked Song first. "Never mind. See you tomorrow."

Autumn waved and grabbed her bag, saying something about a singing lesson before racing off down the hall.

Kensy finished putting away her things. She double-checked she had everything she needed to complete her homework then closed her locker door. As she turned to leave, Kensy spotted Autumn at the other end of the corridor talking to Harper. They were joined by Carlos and seemed to be deep in conversation. It was a bit strange for someone who was in such a tearing hurry just a moment ago. Kensy felt a pang in her chest. Had Autumn made up an excuse not to invite her along? Oddly, Mrs. Vanden Boom appeared and together the group walked through a doorway and out of sight.

A hand on her arm jolted the girl back to the present.

Kensy whirled around to find Inez standing beside her. "Sorry, I didn't mean to jump," she said. "Do you know if Autumn goes to singing lessons with Harper and Carlos?"

"I don't think so," the girl replied, her eyebrows knitting together. "Carlos doesn't have a musical bone in his body, and Harper plays the cello and has lessons in Chelsea on Thursday with the same teacher as me. I don't remember Autumn ever saying anything about singing, though, sorry. Why – do you sing?"

Kensy bit her lip. "Yes," she lied, immediately regretting it.

The word was out of her mouth before she had time to think. Music was probably the one part of her and Max's education that had been sadly neglected. Fitz had taught Max some chords on the guitar, but Kensy had never been that interested in learning an instrument. She could barely remember the words or hold the tune to every new school's song she'd had to learn.

"I can ask my cello teacher to recommend someone if you're looking," Inez offered.

But singing lessons were the furthest thing from Kensy's mind. Was Autumn just pretending to be her friend? Kensy racked her brain for something she might have said to upset the girl, but nothing sprang to mind. She thanked Inez and said goodbye, then rushed off to find her brother.

CHAPTER 15

Kensy hitched her schoolbag higher and pushed her way through the double doors. Dreary gray skies had given way to dusk. She'd always thought the worst thing about the onset of winter was the shortening days; it was going to take some getting used to, especially having come straight from an Australian spring. She looked around for Max and spotted him talking to two senior boys. They were laughing and both shook Max's hand before heading off.

"Who are they?" Kensy asked.

Max greeted her with a winning smile. "The big fellow is Alfie – remember, we saw him when we came for our interview? The other guy is Liam. They were just asking me about this morning."

"Of course they were," Kensy sniped. She glanced about impatiently.

"What's the matter with you?" Max said. "I thought you'd be happy I beat Magoo, and you didn't do too badly out there this afternoon."

The girl shrugged gloomily.

"I haven't stopped thinking about them either, Kens," Max said.

"I know. It's not only that." Kensy had suddenly remembered the note in her pocket. She reached inside and grasped it. Maybe there would be another cryptic clue from their parents today when they got home. Although Max was convinced the notepad was merely a coincidence. She looked up and down the street. "Where's Song? Fitz said he'd be waiting for us."

"He's probably just been held up at home," the boy said. "Do you want to grab something from the corner shop? I'm sure we'll meet him on the way. Fitz gave me five pounds."

"Why didn't he give *me* five pounds?" Kensy grouched. "In that case, yes, I'd like chocolate and lots of it."

The children set off down the street toward the row of shops that started on the corner of Ponsonby Place and wrapped their way around to Ponsonby Terrace. They crossed the street and left their bags on the sidewalk outside the whitewashed newsagency with blue awnings.

A buzzer sounded a sharp alarm as they walked inside, alerting a plump middle-aged woman behind the counter to their presence. It needn't have bothered. The woman was glued to a small television mounted on a wall bracket above and didn't look over despite Kensy saying hello. The girl soon realized that she was one of the three women they'd seen outside the shop yesterday and again that morning across from the school – the smoker with the envelopes.

Max made a beeline for the chocolate aisle. Kensy didn't make it that far; a newspaper on the middle shelf had caught her eye. She looked at the masthead and recognized it to be Fitz's favorite. No matter where they were in the world, he always seemed to have a copy of that paper.

The girl drew a sharp breath. "So that's it," she whispered to herself, an idea forming in her head. Kensy flicked it open to see if she could find any further details on the inside page.

"This is not a library," the woman barked, without breaking her gaze from the television set. "You read it, you buy it."

Kensy squeaked an apology and hurried around to her brother. "*This* is what she does!" she said, shoving the newspaper at him.

"Who?" Max glanced at the front page, then went back to deciding which chocolates to buy.

"Dame Spencer," Kensy said. "When we were at Alexandria and I saw the helicopter fly off, that lighthouse was on the underside of it." She pointed at the masthead, which bore the words "*The Beacon*" and the lighthouse symbol. "Fitz is always reading this paper."

"No wonder she's so rich then, if she's a newspaper baroness," Max said. He still didn't understand why his sister was so excited about it.

"Do you think there could be anything in here about Mum and Dad?" Kensy asked. "If Dame Spencer owns a newspaper, she'd have investigative journalists and foreign correspondents stationed all around the world, at her fingertips. Maybe she can find them!"

"You two all right over there?" The woman's eyes flickered from the television as her program was interrupted by an advertisement. "You'd better not be fillin' your pockets, like all the other little snots round 'ere."

"We're not!" Kensy snapped. She hated being accused of bad behavior for the sole reason that she was a child. Adults did it more than any of them would care to admit.

"Well, I wouldn't put it past you. In my experience, kids are just about good for nothin'," the woman said.

"Geez. Thanks, Mum," a male voice shouted from the floor above them. Max glanced at the moldy ceiling and wondered if there was an apartment up there. "I'm goin' out."

"You'd better get yourself down to Esme's

or you'll be in strife," the woman screeched back. "You know she's got special jobs for you. And if you plan on ever gettin' out of 'ere, you'd better go and do 'em, you lazy, good-for-nothin' sack of spuds."

Kensy's jaw flapped open. She was about to say something when Max touched her arm and shook his head. Rolling her eyes, Kensy took two bars of chocolate from the shelf. Max had amassed a small pile of sweets for himself too. They walked back around to pay for them, dumping the goods onto the counter.

Kensy set the paper off to the side. "I couldn't find an address for the *Beacon*, but we can look it up when we get home. I think we should try to see Dame Spencer after school tomorrow."

The woman's face settled into a sneer as she rang up the items. "Vauxhall Bridge Road," she muttered.

"Sorry, were you talking to us?" Kensy asked.

"Bleedin' 'eck, who else would I be talkin' to?" the woman grouched. She stuck out her chin, which had an unfortunately positioned mole right in the middle that seemed to be sprouting its own head of hair. "The *Beacon* building is just around on the main road – blind Freddy could see it," the woman said. "That poor biddy – you wouldn't want to be her for all the money in the world and she does have more than her fair share of it."

Kensy was surprised to hear the woman had sympathy for anyone. "Why is that?" she asked. This was the last place she thought she'd be getting some answers about Cordelia Spencer.

"So many tragedies in 'er life," the shop-keeper replied, shaking her head. "First, she loses 'er parents – run over by a bus – then 'er 'usband drops dead. And about twelve years ago – I remember 'cause it was the exact same day my 'usband 'ad come 'ome after a long stint away – 'er son and daughter-in-law and nephew are all killed in a plane crash. You wonder what she ever did to deserve all that . . . Mind you, she is a convict."

Max frowned. "A convict?"

"From Australia," the woman whispered,

as though that in itself constituted a criminal offense.

"That's terrible," Max said. "Not that she's from Australia, but all those dreadful things with her family. Does she have anyone left?"

"One son – bit of a peacock, I 'ear." The woman drummed her sausage fingers on the countertop. "Are you buyin' that paper or not? As much as I am the oracle of all wisdom and useful information, I'd prefer to get on wiv my life and not waste my time talkin' to the likes of you two."

Max placed the copy of the *Beacon* in front of her, then counted out the extra change. As he picked up the bag of sweets and Kensy went to take the paper, the woman reached across and grabbed hold of the girl's wrist.

"Are you trying to rob me?" she glowered. "You're five pence short."

Kensy gasped. She pulled back, but the woman's grip was much stronger than she'd expected. "No, of course not," the girl snapped. "Now, let go of me!"

Max quickly rummaged around in his

pocket for the last coin. He found ten pence and swiftly dropped it into the woman's hand. Satisfied, she released Kensy.

"Don't worry about the change," the boy said, as he and his sister scurried from the shop.

Kensy's heart was thumping so hard it felt as though it would burst through her chest. "Do you think she has a giant oven out the back to cook all the children who are five pence short?" she said shakily.

Max grinned. "She does look like she's eaten a few in her time."

Kensy giggled and unwrapped her chocolate bar, regaining her composure. Max popped a handful of malt balls into his mouth.

"Come on," he said. "I'll race you home."

They collected their bags from the sidewalk and ran along the street toward number thirteen. As Max dashed across the road, Kensy accidentally dropped the newspaper. With a grunt of frustration, the girl stopped to gather up the pages. She stepped onto the road just as a black cab pulled away from the curb and hurtled toward her.

Max turned at the sound of squealing of tires. "Look out!" he cried.

Kensy froze for a split second, then came to her senses and bolted out of the way in the nick of time. She leapt onto the sidewalk as the vehicle sped past, clipping the tail of her coat. The driver didn't bother to stop, veering into John Islip Street and disappearing from sight.

A lady pushing a baby carriage rushed to Kensy, who was sprawled on the ground in shock. "Are you all right?" she asked, crouching down. "Oh dear, you're bleeding."

Kensy gingerly pushed herself up off the ground and dusted her uniform. She pulled a tissue from her pocket and pressed it against her grazed knees, grimacing at the touch. "I thought the taxi drivers in London were supposed to be the politest in the world."

"Not that one, apparently." The woman produced a wet wipe from the bag under the baby carriage and handed it to Kensy.

Max stood there staring at the end of the road, wishing he'd thought to look at the number plate. "That driver should have his license taken away," the boy said.

"Would you like me to call someone?" the woman offered.

"It's okay, this is us," Kensy said, pointing to the glossy black door before them.

The woman frowned. "Really? I thought that house was empty most of the time. I'm Claudia, by the way. I just live down the street."

The front door swung open and Song stepped out onto the tiny bridge that linked the house to the sidewalk. He was straightening his tie and smoothing his hair. "Miss Kensington!" he gasped, and sprinted onto the sidewalk. "What happened?"

"She was almost mown down by some maniac cab driver," Max replied. As if things weren't hard enough at the moment. He knew his sister was tough, but it must have given her quite a shock.

Looking slightly rattled, Song gave Kensy the once-over. "I should have come to meet you. I am so sorry, Miss Kensington, I had an unexpected visitor," he said with grave sincerity, looking as if he were about to cry. "Are you hurt?"

The girl shook her head and was quickly bundled off inside with the promise of antiseptic and gauze.

"Thanks again," Max said to Claudia. He looked at the pram, which was covered by a cloth hiding the baby from view. "What's its name?" he asked.

The woman blinked and looked at him blankly.

"May I see?" he said, pointing at the pram. "I love babies."

"Oh," Claudia said, laughing. "Perhaps next time. She's sleeping and I really don't like to disturb her. She's not easy." She cast a nervous glance at the pram.

"Next time then," Max said with a smile. He picked up his schoolbag and walked toward the door of number thirteen Ponsonby Terrace. Today had been a lot of things, but uneventful was certainly not one of them.

CHAPTER 16

XK RKBUMBZQBA SFPFQLO

Max closed the front door behind him, careful not to let in the stray leaves the icy wind had rustled up. He was about to head upstairs when a funny feeling came over him. He turned and looked around the sitting room, setting his bag down on the floor. Something was different. Max was trying to think what it was when he spotted an object poking out from under one of the cream sofas. He walked closer and saw that it was a triangular piece of porcelain. Max picked it up and turned it over. The other side was patterned in white and royal blue, and he remembered seeing a large vase with that same floral detail inside the entrance hall. Max ducked down to see if there was anything else hiding under there but came up empty-handed.

He walked back to collect his bag and found that the vase had gone. He also noticed the rug was askew, as if a tango dancer had come through, and a painting on the wall was ever so slightly off kilter. Deep in thought, Max walked upstairs and changed into sweatpants and a navy sweater. He gathered up his homework and made his way to the kitchen, where Kensy was perched on the end of the table. Song was wearing surgical gloves and a mask as he applied antiseptic and bandages to the girl's knees.

"I didn't realize there'd be an operating room down here," the boy said, stifling a grin.

"One can never be too careful about germs," Song replied, his words coming out as one long muffled sentence.

Max placed his books on the other end of the table and sat down. "That's true. You don't know what you might catch from Kensy."

"Ha ha, you are *such* a comedian," the girl retorted. She poked out her tongue, then winced as Song swabbed the last of the grazes.

Wellie and Mac watched the goings-on from the basket they shared by the range.

"So did your unexpected visitor have anything to do with this?" Max pulled the triangle of porcelain out from his pile of books.

Kensy shot him a questioning look.

Song squeezed his eyes shut for a second, as if replaying something in his mind. He removed the surgical mask. "Where did you find that, Master Maxim?"

"Under the cream sofa," the boy said, opening up one of his books. He turned to a fresh page and took up his pen.

Song returned his focus to Kensy's grazes. "How careless of me. I cannot believe I knocked over the vase while I was vacuuming. At least now I will be able to put it back together."

Max thought it must have been one heck of a collision for the piece to have flown all the way from the entrance hall to the far side of the sitting room. "I hope it wasn't too valuable," the boy said.

"As if," Kensy replied. With Song's seal of approval, she shuffled down to the floor. "I don't think you'll find anything from a discount store in this house."

"How are your knees feeling now, Miss Kensington?" Song asked, changing the subject. He removed his gloves and deposited them into a pedal bin.

"Throbbing," the girl replied. "But I'll live. I don't even think I'll have a scar." She sounded somewhat disappointed by the fact. "Not like this," she said, and opened her left palm for the butler to see a faint pink line spanning two inches.

Song nodded. "That *is* impressive. Might I know how you acquired it?"

"I sliced it open while ice-skating last year. I thought Max was going to be sick – you should have seen all the blood, but I didn't even cry," Kensy said proudly.

Max rolled his eyes. "Yes, you did."

"Only when Mum gave me that massive needle so she could stitch me up," the girl said defensively.

Song looked impressed. "Your mother did that work?"

"Our mother is a doctor," Kensy explained. "She always fixes us up, and Dad and Fitz like to think they're amateur dentists too. We've never been to another doctor or a real dentist, which is probably quite a bad thing to admit." She felt a pang at the thought of her mother and father.

Max did too.

"It sounds like they are all very skilled. Anyway," Song said brightly, clasping his hands. "I have a carrot cake with cream cheese frosting for your afternoon tea and I will get my famous hot chocolate underway." He took the saucepan out of the cupboard and placed it onto the island.

"Yum," Kensy said, making an effort to perk up. "I think I'll go and get changed first."

She disappeared upstairs, leaving Song and Max alone with the dogs.

"Who was your unexpected visitor?" Max asked. He pretended to read the list of questions he had for English homework.

"Someone who should know better than to go poking their nose into other people's business," Song replied. He wriggled his own nose with his fingers, grimacing at the touch.

Max watched the man carefully. There was more to it than that – he was sure of it. The shadow under Song's left eye would seem to indicate that housework was a contact sport.

* * *

Kensy stared at the notepaper in her hands. It was silly to have thought there would be another message today, if that's what this even was, but she still couldn't help feeling a bubble of disappointment rise in her throat. She brushed away the tears that threatened to fall and summoned the steely resolve her parents would be proud of. Kensy refolded the page and returned it to her pocket for safekeeping. Perhaps there would be something tomorrow.

She was about to draw the curtains when a movement in the house across the street caught her eye. A woman dressed in a leopard-print leotard and black footless tights was jumping about, dancing and kicking her legs high in the air. At one point, she performed a backflip, followed by a handstand and a cartwheel. Mesmerized, Kensy leaned closer until her breath began to fog the window. The woman had to be a professional gymnast or a dancer. Kensy was still staring when, for a brief moment, their eyes met. The girl gasped and took a step back in surprise. The woman looked equally as shocked and hurriedly drew the curtains shut. Kensy could have sworn it was the elderly lady with purple hair she'd seen outside the corner shop. But that couldn't be right – that woman was positively ancient and her back curved like a parabola.

Kensy couldn't wait to tell Max what she'd just seen. She threw her uniform on the floor and hunted about for something to wear. Although it was just over a day since they'd arrived in London, the entire contents of her wardrobe had made its way onto the floor, the chair or the end of her bed. As she carefully stepped into a pair of jeans and shrugged on a navy-and-white striped top, Kensy wondered if Song was the telling off type. She probably should try to tidy up, but there was homework to be done. She'd do it later.

Kensy was about to gather up her books when a peculiar thing happened. Her watch vibrated. It had never done that before. Kensy peered at the dial as it vibrated again and then for a third time. She hoped it wasn't broken, especially seeing as though she and Max had only just gotten them for their last birthday.

Suddenly, a thought dawned on the girl – a flash of hope. Kensy grabbed her things and hurtled down the stairs. Maybe Max's watch had vibrated too. Maybe, just maybe, this was the message she had been waiting for all day.

CHAPTER 17

QEB JLOMBQE XOJP

Bundled in their woolen coats, Song and the children bustled out the front door and onto the sidewalk. Wellie and Mac trotted ahead on their navy leads, sporting identical coats in navy-and-red tartan. They were on their way to dinner, as Song had arranged for the locks to be changed. Apparently, there had been a string of robberies in the area, though Max wondered if it had more to do with Song's unexpected visitor than any petty thefts.

Kensy and Max walked beside one another in stony silence. They had just had a fight and neither of them was ready to make up yet. In all her excitement, Kensy had told her brother about her watch and the geriatric gymnast across the road, and hadn't appreciated him laughing in her face and telling her she was imagining things yet again.

The group turned left at the end of the street and were treated to a view of the River Thames on the other side of a busy four-lane road.

"I see the dogs have taken a shine to you both," Song said, in an effort to liven the mood. "They are very fussy when it comes to giving their affections. Any love they have for me is only on account of the fact that I feed them."

"If the dogs belong to Dame Spencer, why doesn't she take them with her when she comes to the city?" Kensy asked.

"Allergies," Song replied with a sigh.

Max's brow furrowed. "But if she's allergic, why does she have them at all? That doesn't seem right," he said, earning a growl from both terriers.

"Oh no, not Dame Spencer," Song said, shaking his head. "Her butler."

Kensy frowned. "Hang on, I'm confused. I thought you were her butler?"

"At Alexandria, but not here in the city," Song said, as if it were the most obvious conclusion.

Kensy glanced at her brother. A silent message passed between them and their fight was forgotten. "Song, could you take us to meet her tomorrow?" the girl asked. "We know her office is nearby on the main road."

"We want to thank her for letting us stay in her house," Max chimed in.

"Well . . . Dame Spencer is a very busy woman," the butler said hesitantly. He noted the looks of disappointment on the children's faces and quickly added, "But I will see what I can do."

Literally just around the corner from Ponsonby Terrace, Song and the children walked the short distance to an establishment called The Morpeth Arms, where they would be having dinner. It sat on the corner of another row of Georgian terraces, wrapping its way around into Ponsonby Place. Baskets of red geraniums decorated the frontage along with planter boxes bursting with blooms. It was an impressive display considering it was almost winter. Song pushed open one of the front doors and shepherded the twins and dogs into the pub.

The atmosphere was as warm as the temperature inside, with several tables occupied by locals and business people alike, unwinding at the end of their busy days. A jolly man with a round face and smiling blue eyes gave Song a wave from behind the bar. Wellie and Mac wagged their tails at high speed as a young woman rushed through from a back room.

"Hello, babies," she cooed. "I've missed you two." She ruffled their furry heads. "Hello, Song, hi, kids," she said, then took the dogs' leads and promptly disappeared with them.

"Miss Kensington, Master Maxim, this is my good friend Gary," Song said, introducing them to the friendly barman. "And that whirlwind of a girl was Stephie – she will look after Wellington and Mackintosh while we have our dinner. They are not allowed upstairs in the restaurant."

"Hiya, kids," the fellow said with a wave.

"I've saved the best spot in the house for you. But before I show you to your table, I'm going to take you on a grand tour of the cells downstairs."

"Cells?" the twins said in unison. Both of them thought Gary must have meant the cellar.

Max spotted a television screen in the corner of the room and a sign underneath that read CAN YOU SEE OUR GHOST? He nudged Kensy. "I wonder if it's got anything to do with that."

Song made a face. "I am sure that Master Maxim and Miss Kensington would love your special tour, but I am afraid it may give them nightmares – especially if you happen to run into anyone down there."

Kensy giggled. "Max might be scared, but I'll be fine. I don't have nightmares."

"That's not true," her brother grumbled under his breath.

"Fantastic!" Gary exclaimed. "Follow me."

The barman steered the children through to a back room, where they descended a steep, narrow staircase. Song opted to stay behind. Downstairs, the air was cloying and musty, and the twins both felt an immediate drop in temperature.

Kensy's mouth gaped open as she looked around. "There *are* cells."

Max peered into one of the tiny spaces. They were only a few square feet at most, with a curved brick ceiling. Even he couldn't stand up inside without having to stoop.

"They're so small," Kensy observed. "It wouldn't be very comfortable to sleep in there – I mean, your bed would hardly fit."

"No beds, I'm afraid. And not just one prisoner. Anything up to fifteen adults would be crammed into that space," Gary said somberly. "It was a horrid business."

Max's eyes widened. "But why were they kept here? I can't imagine that many people in the pub were so badly behaved they had to be locked up."

Gary roared with laughter and admitted he'd considered housing some of his rowdier patrons down there on more than one occasion, except that the bars to keep people locked in were missing these days. He explained that there had once been a huge prison further up the road. It was eventually closed in 1890 and now a magnificent museum called the Tate Gallery stands in its stead. But in the old days, it was a much darker place and The Morpeth Arms had served as the officers' local watering hole.

Gary told them, from a bird's-eye view, the prison looked like a flower – with six penta-gonal buildings around a central hexagon. The plans were rather beautiful, but the reality of the prison was far from it. There were tunnels beneath the jail and one of them led to the cells under the pub. The officers used it to herd inmates downstairs if there was an overflow from the prison, or they would march them under the roadways and hold prisoners there before they were brought up to be loaded on the convict ships that were bound for Australia. Apparently, the better classes of Londoners weren't keen to see riffraff on the streets.

A shadow passed across the wall and Max jumped into the air. "Did you see that?" he asked the others.

Kensy spun around, hoping to catch a

glimpse.

"I think you may have just spied one of our friendly ghosts," Gary said, grinning. "Or it might have been the cat bounding about on the stairs back there – she's probably been spooked by Wellie and Mac. They are not friends."

Nonetheless, a shiver ran down Kensy's spine and she clutched her brother's arm.

"I thought you said you weren't scared," Max said. He'd never admit it, but he was quite glad she was holding on to him, even if the shadow did belong to the cat.

"I'm not," the girl said. "I'm just cold, that's all."

"Do the tunnels still exist?" Max asked.

"I imagine they do, but you'd have to dig through there to find them," Gary said. He led the children along the row of cells which came to an abrupt end with a brick wall. "This whole area is a labyrinth. They've uncovered a few bits and pieces when there's been building work, but unless a house comes down, they tend to leave things alone. English Heritage has enough to do without looking for more work."

Max ran his hand over the cool bricks. In one of the cells, he found a name that had been carved into the wall. He wondered who Henry Ball was and what he'd done to end up there. His mind turned to his parents. What if they were somewhere suffering a similar fate? There may have been a couple of hundred years and some thousands of miles between what had happened here and where his parents were in Africa, but the boy couldn't help thinking about the possible parallels.

* * *

The children trekked back upstairs behind Gary, but instead of stopping at the pub level, they continued on up another couple of flights to a beautiful dining room. Decorated in rich red wallpaper with sepia photographs and other artworks, there was a fireplace and side tables adorned with lamps. It reminded Kensy of Dame Spencer's house in the countryside, although the pieces here showed quite a bit more wear and tear. Apart from a couple sitting on the other side of the room, the restaurant was empty.

Gary ushered the children to their table, which was perpendicular to one of three floor-to-ceiling double-hung windows overlooking the river. Instead of individual chairs, there was an elegant button-upholstered double lounge seat on either side of the table.

"Welcome to the Spying Room," Gary announced, and handed each of the children a pair of binoculars.

"What?" Kensy screwed up her nose as she shuffled into her seat by the window.

Max sat down and peered outside. "Whoa! You can see MI6 right across there, lit up like a Christmas tree." He turned to Gary. "So, we're allowed to spy on the spies? Is that why it's called the Spying Room?"

Gary nodded. "Not just allowed – I strongly encourage it. You never know what you might learn by sitting here."

Song appeared in the doorway. "I see you have Miss Kensington and Master Maxim on the hunt already," he said with an amused grin.

"Have you ever seen anything interesting?" Kensy asked. She tried to get a peek inside the glass-fronted building while Max adjusted the focus on his binoculars.

"Well, here's the thing," Gary began. "In all the years I've been managing this establishment, I've seen the lights go on and off – same with the computers. I've seen people on the balconies, but I've never once spotted a human being inside that building."

The twins put down their binoculars and stared at him.

"Are you sure?" Kensy said. She gazed at the building with renewed interest. It reminded her a little of a Mayan temple.

The manager nodded and crossed his heart. "Same goes for every other person working here. Anyway, I should let you have a gander at what you'd like for your dinner."

"Why don't you join us?" Song suggested.

The man protested that he didn't want to intrude, but the children practically begged him to stay. They were dying to hear more of his stories. Gary finally agreed, and the group placed their orders. Kensy opted for a burger while Max and Gary chose the cod and chips. Song selected a sirloin steak, medium rare. It seemed like no time before their meals arrived.

"So, how was your first day at school?" Song asked.

"It was good," Kensy said, munching on a fistful of fries. "We made lots of friends, which is always a bit surprising on your first day, although I'm not sure about a few of them."

Max frowned at her, wondering what she was getting at. He'd ask her later. "Some of the teachers are hilarious," he said, and soon had them all in stitches reenacting Mr. Reffell's impersonation of Lord Nelson.

"Do you know the lady who owns the newsagency at the end of the street?" Kensy asked, once they'd exhausted their school stories. "She's awful. I wouldn't be surprised if she had a giant oven out the back reserved for children."

"Ah, that would be Mrs. Grigsby," Song said with a nod. "She is undeniably the meanest woman I know."

"Wait till you meet her son, Derek," Gary added. "He has a diamanté earring the size of a pigeon's egg and more gold chains than the mayor of London. He's also partial to wearing his pants halfway down his backside. He got himself a new tattoo recently and, I must say, I laughed out loud when I saw he had the word 'genius' on his forearm spelled with a 'J.'"

Max collapsed into a fit of giggles. "You're making that up!"

"I wish I was," Gary said, shaking his head.

"Derek is not what we would consider the sharpest tool in the shed," Song agreed. "But don't worry, Mrs. Grigsby will leave you alone when she realizes you are with me. I take her dumplings whenever I am in London, though she always complains there are never enough. That is because she is very greedy."

"I'm sure that's true. And why would you take her anything?" Kensy asked, appalled.

"Confucius says keep your friends close and your enemies closer," Song said, waving his steak knife in the air.

Max cocked his head to one side. "I thought that was either Machiavelli or Sun Tzu or maybe it was from a movie."

Song pursed his lips. "Hmm, you are much

too clever for an eleven-year-old," he said with mock displeasure.

"I am too," Kensy told the table. "I beat Max in the spelling bee this year."

"I am in no doubt of that," Song said with a decisive nod. "You are twins, and twins are always as smart as one another. Except when one twin is much smarter and better looking."

Kensy glanced up sharply, ready to take exception, while her brother winked cheekily and said, "I know exactly what you mean."

CHAPTER 18

GBKFRP

Max had woken early, as usual. Through the open curtains, he lay in his bed watching the last of the stars fade and hoped they'd see some sun today. Endless hours of gray wasn't good for anyone's mood. He couldn't help thinking that the convicts got the better deal being sent to Australia. At least there were blue skies most of the time – even in winter.

Although the children did their best to convince Song they could make their own way to school, the butler insisted on tagging along. Besides, he argued, Wellie and Mac needed a walk.

Kensy barreled out the front door with Max behind her. She was still upset about the conversation she'd had with Song over breakfast. Another attempt to persuade him to take them to the *Beacon* offices to see Dame Spencer had failed. Kensy had tried every trick in the book and had even appealed to the man's impeccable sense of decorum by reasoning that it would be rude to not meet the person who was so generously hosting them, but the butler had remained steadfastly evasive and promised nothing.

Kensy looked up and was surprised to see the old woman with purple hair standing on the sidewalk opposite. She was sure it was the same person she'd seen doing flips and kicks yesterday afternoon. As Kensy had recalled, the woman's back was bent and she was leaning heavily on her cane. She didn't look as though she'd make it to the end of the road let alone put on an acrobatic display. Kensy tried not to stare in case the woman spotted her. She was still burning with embarrassment over having been caught spying.

A noisy car coughed and rattled into the street, pulling up outside the old woman's house.

Max nudged his sister as a young man wearing a New York Yankees cap backward, and with enough bling to light up the night sky, hauled himself out of the driver's seat. "Do you think that might be Derek?"

"You mean the genius with a 'J'?" Kensy quipped.

The fellow's outfit was pure gangster with low-riding jeans deliberately showcasing his underpants, high-top sneakers and a tight black T-shirt that was presumably designed to show off the wearer's physique – except this guy's muscles were well hidden.

Song glanced across the road as he pulled the front door closed. "Hello, Derek," he called, confirming the children's suspicions.

"Hiya, Song," the man called back, his chains jangling. They clearly set Wellie and Mac's nerves on edge, as both pups had begun a guttural growl. "Can you bring me mam some of your dumplins? They always put her in a better mood."

"I will see what I can manage," Song replied with a polite nod. He waved to the old woman with purple hair. "Good morning, Mrs. Brightside."

She smiled and gave a friendly wave, wobbling dangerously on her cane. "Lovely to 'ave you back, Song darlin'. You must pop round for a cuppa."

"That is very kind of you to offer," Song said. He began to usher Kensy and Max, who were busy gawping at Derek's car down the road. "Come along, children, we'd better get going."

The lad's iridescent green hatchback bore little resemblance to its original manufactured shape, having been lowered almost to the ground with huge silver rims that barely fitted inside the wheel arches. The doors opened upward like a fancy sports car, and the window tinting was so dark you couldn't see inside, not to mention the whale tail on the back. Despite the obvious investment of cash, the car looked cheap and nasty, a lot like its owner.

Kensy and Max did their best not to gawk, but Derek was the most fascinating creature they'd seen in days. He walked around to the back of the car and opened the hatch, which was lined with a blue tarpaulin – not at all in keeping with the exterior sparkle. It almost looked as if he'd been using the car to cart rubble. What was more interesting to Kensy, though, was that the old lady greeted the young man with a good crack on the head with her handbag.

"Where were you last night?" she demanded.

"Ow!" Derek complained as the old woman grabbed him by the ear. "I was busy."

"Don't you let me down again." Mrs. Brightside pinched his arm for good measure, causing Derek to yelp for a second time. "We're on a tight schedule, you know."

Kensy giggled behind her hand. "What do you think that was about?"

"I suspect Derek was meant to do some jobs for Mrs. Brightside, but he is not the most reliable worker," Song said. "She is a good friend of Mrs. Grigsby."

"Is she just as mean?" Max asked. From the woman's previous exchange with Song, he didn't imagine so.

"I have always found her to be quite delightful," Song said, as he and the children walked along the street with Wellie and Mac sniffing everything in their paths.

"Does anyone else live at her house?" Kensy asked.

"No, she is a widow," Song said. "Why do you ask?"

Kensy was about to tell him what she'd seen the previous day when she spotted Autumn at the end of the road. "Never mind," she said, and ran ahead to catch up to her.

When they'd arrived home from dinner last night, Max had asked her what she'd meant when she said she wasn't sure about a few of their new friends. He'd told her she was being silly and, when Kensy thought about it, she was inclined to agree. Autumn had been nothing but lovely, as had Carlos and Harper. None of them deserved her ridiculous suspicions.

"Bye, Song! Bye, puppies! See you this afternoon!" Kensy called over her shoulder.

"It's all right, Song, I'll walk with you," Max said. There was something about the butler that made him feel safe and calm.

"Thank you, Master Maxim." Song nodded. "May I ask if there is something troubling you? Confucius says a trouble shared is a trouble halved – or perhaps that was my mother who told me that."

Max exhaled. "How long do you have?"

"I would listen for as long as you need, but I think we will run short of time with school not far away," Song replied.

"I'm worried about Mum and Dad," the boy admitted. "I don't say that to Kensy, of course, because I don't want her to worry. We tell each other they're fine, but, really, how could a notepad on Kensy's bedside table prove that?"

Song's brow creased. "A notepad on the bedside table?"

"Kensy believes it's a sign from Mum, but it's probably just a coincidence," Max explained.

Song, Max and the dogs rounded the corner and were swept up in a wave of children heading toward the school.

"Hey, Max, hi, Song!" Sachin shouted from further down the street. He ran over to them, his backpack jostling up and down on his shoulders.

Wellie and Mac sniffed the boy's trousers.

"They like you," Max said.

Sachin grinned. "Of course they do. What's not to like?"

"Do you and Song know each other?" Max asked. He was sure that Sachin had called both their names.

Song glanced at Sachin then back at Max. "I met Master Sachin when I was out walking Wellington and Mackintosh one morning. The dogs took a shine to him right away and I instantly knew he must be a very good boy."

"I've run into Song and the dogs a few times since then. We're old friends now, aren't we?" Sachin said, giving each of the dogs a hefty pat.

"Is it okay if Sachin and I walk the rest of the way together?" Max asked Song.

The man nodded. "I will meet you here this afternoon."

Max smiled and pushed up his spectacles. "Thanks, Song. You're one of the good guys."

"I am the best one of the good guys," Song replied, patting the boy on the shoulder and looking quite pleased.

Max knelt down and ruffled Wellie and Mac's heads. "See you two later," he said. The pups wagged their tails.

"Those dogs are so cute," Sachin said, as he and Max strode off.

Song raised his head ever so slightly and, unbeknown to Max, Sachin turned and gave an almost imperceptible nod.

CHAPTER 19

PEBISBA

The twins' first lesson of the day was English and this morning Miss Witherbee was wound up like a clock. When Yasmina asked her a question about the text they were reading, the woman almost took the poor girl's head off, saying that she, of all people, should know what to do. Kensy wondered exactly what that meant and why Yasmina should know when everyone else seemed to be in the dark about things.

The children took out their copies of *Swallows and Amazons* and were ordered to read the whole of chapter eight in complete silence. When they were finished, they were to answer a page of comprehension questions. Kensy thought it must be a test and that maybe she'd missed that part of the instruction because Miss Witherbee was patrolling the room like a commandant. As she passed by Kensy's desk, the teacher exploded.

"If you can't keep quiet, Miss Grey, you will have to sit on your own," the woman boomed, startling the rest of the class.

Kensy looked at her in disbelief. "But I didn't say a word, Miss Witherbee," she protested. She could feel the heat rising to her cheeks, and hated herself for it. What was it with the adults around here? Mrs. Grigsby yesterday and now Miss Witherbee – both accusing her of things she hadn't done.

"Such impertinence!" Miss Witherbee seethed. "Do you want to argue with me? I think you'll find that, as a former captain of the Oxbridge debating team, I'm a more than worthy opponent."

Kensy was about to say something else when she caught sight of her brother pressing a finger to his lips and shaking his head. Kensy rolled her eyes, which Miss Witherbee fortunately didn't catch.

"What's wrong with her?" Kensy whispered to Yasmina.

The girl shrugged. "I don't know. She's not usually as grumpy as this."

Willow Witherbee spun around. "I heard someone speaking. Who was it?"

Her outburst was met with stunned silence.

"I know what I heard. It was you, wasn't it?" She pointed a skinny manicured finger at Kensy.

The girl swallowed hard. She didn't want to own up, but she wasn't about to tell on Yasmina either. "Yes, Miss Witherbee," Kensy mumbled.

"Right, stand up. You can go and sit over there." The teacher pointed to a desk at the back of the room, facing the wall underneath shelves loaded with large reference books and the entire Harry Potter series. "If you'd rather spend the rest of the morning with the headmaster, that can be arranged."

Kensy sighed and gathered her things together. Maybe Mr. MacGregor would be more reasonable, although the thought of being put on Kevin duty, catching flies to feed his beloved plant (if that was even true), didn't thrill her too much either. Kensy sat down at the desk and began to reread the passage. English was one of her best subjects and she was determined not to let Miss Witherbee get the better of her. She'd only been sitting there a couple of minutes when there was a loud crack and the whole class looked up from their books.

Yasmina turned around. "Kensy!" she shouted, as the shelf above the girl seemed to split in half.

Instinctively, Kensy shielded her face. An avalanche of books rained down, toppling the girl off her chair before she managed to roll away. Max was out of his seat in seconds. He grabbed Kensy and helped her to her feet as the books continued to thump down onto the floor, scattering everywhere. But that wasn't the last of the drama. The broken shelf shot across the room, narrowly missing Yasmina and some of the other children.

"Oh no!" Miss Witherbee gasped. "Are you all right, Kensy?"

The girl had a bump on her head from where the first book had connected, but apart from that she was just a little shaken up.

"Looks like someone sawed the shelf almost in half," Sachin said, holding up the board in question. "The weight of the books must have caused it to crack."

"Imagine having that on your gravestone. Killed by *Harry Potter and the Order of the Phoenix*, hardback edition," Sachin joked, then grimaced. "Too soon?"

Kensy managed a small laugh. "Gee, thanks."

"My goodness, who would do such a thing?" Miss Witherbee squawked, holding her cheeks with both hands.

Max's ears were ringing. He couldn't help but wonder if the woman's protest was a tad overwrought.

There was a knock on the door and Mr. MacGregor poked his head around. "Good heavens, what's gone on in here?" he asked, entering the room.

"We're absolutely fine, Mr. MacGregor," Miss Witherbee said quickly. Her eyes darted about and she didn't seem to know what to do with her hands.

Sachin held up the offending piece of lumber. "Someone tried to kill Kensy."

"Don't be ridiculous," Miss Witherbee rebuked. "We have no idea how it happened and asinine speculation is certainly not helpful. I'm sure it was an unfortunate accident, that's all."

Mr. MacGregor walked over to take a look. "This does appear to have a blade mark in it," he said, his eyebrows stitched together in grave concern. "Are you all right, Kensy?" The man examined her forehead, which bore a red blotch and a bit of swelling. "I think you'd better accompany me to the office; Mrs. Potts can arrange an ice pack."

"May I come too, sir?" Max asked.

"Yes, of course," the man said. He turned to Miss Witherbee. "Why don't you have the children stack the books on the cupboard over there and I'll get Mr. Lazenby to take a look at fixing the shelf?"

The woman nodded vigorously and turned her eyes to the floor. "Yes, sir."

And with that, Mr. MacGregor ushered Kensy and Max out the door.

Max looked at Kensy as they walked along the hall to the headmaster's office. "You know it was just an accident, right?"

"Of course it was," Kensy said sarcastically. "Just like the taxi that nearly ran me over on the way home yesterday. Two silly coincidences."

Magoo turned around. "What happened on the way home?" he asked, frowning.

"Some maniac in a taxi almost knocked Kensy down when we were crossing the street. He probably didn't see her," Max said. "It was getting dark."

But Magoo MacGregor wasn't so sure about that. Perhaps the twins needed closer monitoring, he thought to himself. Carlos and Max seemed to have struck up a friendship already, and Autumn and Kensy were a good match too. He knew he could rely on both of them. He'd call them in for a chat as soon as he could.

CHAPTER 20

Sachin and Max walked down the hall, the smell of lunch drawing the students like a line of ants toward the cafeteria. Kensy and Autumn were still putting away their things after their last lesson with Mrs. Vanden Boom. At least there hadn't been any more mishaps and Kensy's headache had dulled. Truth was, she felt fine on the outside, but inside her stomach was churning. More than ever, she wanted her mum and dad, and Fitz too. Being at school kept her mind busy for the most part; it was in the quiet moments that the reality of the situation almost overwhelmed the girl. But there was no giving up. Her parents were alive. She was certain of it.

"Do you have any advanced lessons today?" Kensy asked as they headed to lunch.

Autumn shook her head. "No, I'm in the same classes as you all day."

Kensy smiled. "I'm glad. You're one of those people I feel like I've known forever, which is silly, of course."

Autumn linked arms with the girl. "It's funny, but from the moment I saw you I just knew we were going to get along."

The girls passed by Lola and Misha, who immediately began whispering behind their hands.

"Just ignore those two," Autumn said loudly. "They don't have a brain between them."

"You think you're so clever, Autumn," Lola spat. "But you're not."

"Yeah, not clever," Misha repeated.

"See what I mean? One brain, same thoughts," Autumn said with a shrug.

Kensy couldn't help herself and gave them a death stare – a skill she'd perfected on Max and had occasionally used on mean kids at school. It had the desired effect – Lola poked her tongue out, then scurried away with Misha in tow.

Kensy and Autumn grinned at one another.

"What's it like being a twin?" Autumn asked.

"It's good most of the time. I always have someone to talk to and Max is fun to hang out with and he's really brave and kind." Kensy stopped. "Gee, I shouldn't talk him up too much. Don't tell him I said any of that or his head will get even bigger than it's been since he beat Mr. MacGregor in the race."

"He's handsome too," Autumn said, then clamped her hands over her mouth. A bright-crimson wash crept across her face.

Kensy wrinkled her nose. "Really?"

Fortunately, Kensy left it at that. Relieved, Autumn thought she'd gotten away with it – until they reached the door of the cafeteria.

Kensy raised her eyebrows at Autumn, whose cheeks still looked as though they'd been set alight. "He's never had a girlfriend, you know."

Autumn groaned and covered her face with her hands. "Can you forget I said anything? We're way too young for all that, anyway."

"For now." Kensy grinned. "Come on, I'm starving and the shepherd's pie smells delicious."

The girls joined the queue behind Harper and Inez, who were deep in conversation about an upcoming debating competition. Sachin and Dante were further ahead talking about football, which Kensy kept having to remind herself meant soccer in England. Dante, it seemed, was a Chelsea fan while Sachin followed Manchester United. Both were arguing passionately about last night's game.

Kensy reached the head of the queue, where Mrs. Trimm, the chief dinner lady, was serving up plates of food.

"Hello, dear. I heard you got yourself a bump on the head in English class, of all places," the woman said sympathetically.

Kensy was surprised at how fast news traveled around the school. "I'm fine, really," she replied, putting on a brave face.

"We're a caring school, my love. If there's anything I can do to make life that little bit easier, you just let me know." Elva Trimm gave the girl a wink along with an extra-large helping of pie and lots of melted cheese from the top of the mashed potato.

"That's very kind, thank you," Kensy said. Mrs. Trimm's smile was like a warm hug on a chilly day.

She and Autumn took their lunch and made their way over to sit with Carlos and Max, who had saved them seats.

"If I had a grandmother, I'd want her to be just like Mrs. Trimm," Kensy announced, setting her tray on the table.

Elva Trimm watched as Kensy sat down opposite her brother. The woman had been at the school such a long time now. She was due to retire but could never quite bring herself to do it. Eric Lazenby appeared at the counter. He'd been around as long as Elva.

"Lovely kids, those two," Eric said with a grin.

"So like their dad, it's uncanny," Elva said, and sniffled into her hanky.

Eric gave the woman's arm a squeeze. "They'll be fine with us, love. You know they will."

CHAPTER 21

QEB YBXZLK

True to his word, Song was waiting outside the school gates, with Wellie and Mac sitting like Roman statues in a patch of afternoon sunshine. The temperature hadn't fallen too low just yet, although the West Highland terriers were again wearing their tartan coats. Children spilled through the gates in all directions.

Song squinted into the distance and spotted the twins walking toward him with their friends Autumn and Carlos.

"Oh dear, Miss Kensington. You are having a horrible run of luck," the man said, clucking his tongue. "Mr. MacGregor telephoned to let me know about the accident. How are you feeling?"

Kensy shrugged. "Okay, I guess. It's not too big a bump." The girl touched her forehead and winced slightly. She was probably going to have a bruise the size of Botswana.

"Have you heard from Fitz?" Max asked. He tried to keep his voice light for his sister's sake.

"Not yet, Master Maxim, though no news could be good news." Song paused, as if thinking about how to phrase what he wanted to say next. "Shall we go straight home? I have made scones for afternoon tea and there is jam and cream too. You are welcome to join us," he said to Carlos and Autumn. "I am sure that Miss Kensington and Master Maxim would enjoy some company other than me – I am old and not so much fun."

"I would love to, but I have a piano lesson," Autumn said, taking her cue to leave.

"And it's football training for me," Carlos added.

The pair swiftly said their goodbyes and headed off.

"Please, can we see Dame Spencer?" Max said, turning to the butler.

Song shook his head. "I am afraid she is out of the office this afternoon. We will go another time."

The children shared a look. Neither of them believed a word of it, but there was no point arguing.

The man called Wellie and Mac to attention and, together, the odd group walked home. Song did his best to engage Kensy in conversation, asking her all manner of details about her unfortunate incident. Max lagged behind. He felt edgy. Ever since Kensy had almost been run down by the taxi, he found himself paying particular attention to the vehicles. Trouble was, they were everywhere. Max seemed to have added an extra layer of foreboding to his already uneasy feelings about his parents and he didn't like it one bit.

When they reached number thirteen, the children went upstairs to get changed while Song set off to prepare their afternoon tea.

"He's lying, you know," Kensy said to her

brother in the upstairs hall. "Why doesn't he want us to meet her?"

Max shrugged. "Who knows anything these days?"

The children disappeared into their rooms and Kensy quickly changed out of her uniform. She hurried back downstairs, where Wellie and Mac were sitting in the front hall, still dressed in their coats. Kensy glanced at the entrance and realized that the broken vase had been replaced by a tall porcelain lighthouse, its beacon clear inside the top level. She wondered if . . .

Kensy looked at the dogs. Their leads were hanging on a coat hook by the door. Without a second thought, she grabbed the leads and snapped them onto their collars. "Do you want to go and see Dame Spencer?" she whispered.

The pups wagged their tails and danced about at her feet.

"I'm just taking the dogs for a walk," Kensy said out loud, though quieter than she usually would. She looked at Wellie and Mac and shrugged. "See? I told someone – it's not my fault if they didn't hear me."

The girl unlocked the front door and tiptoed outside, making sure to shut it gently behind her.

Minutes later, Max trotted downstairs to the kitchen, the smell of hot chocolate tantalizing his nostrils. He'd heard Kensy leave her room and expected to see her at the table devouring afternoon tea.

"I presume that you are a fan of jam and cream with your scones," Song said. He deposited a plate on the table and waited for Max to sit down.

"Yes," the boy said distractedly. "Sorry, thank you." He looked over at Wellie and Mac's empty baskets and wondered where the dogs had gotten to. They didn't often stray far from Song.

"Are you going to sit down, Master Maxim?" Song asked, watching the boy shift his weight from one leg to the other.

Max nodded. "I'm a bit cold – I'll just get a sweater," the lad said, and dashed from the room. But he had no intention of doing that at all. If his instincts were correct, his sister had done something even more impulsive than usual.

* * *

Max raced to the end of Ponsonby Terrace and turned left into John Islip Street, heading for the main road. He turned right and sprinted past a quaint pub called The White Swan, running toward the tallest building on the block. He could see the lighthouse symbol on top of it. Mrs. Grigsby was right when she said that blind Freddy wouldn't miss it.

Gasping for air, Max peered through the glass doors and spotted his sister waiting in the reception area with Wellie and Mac. He was about to enter the building when a security guard stopped him in his tracks.

"Where do you think you're going, young man?" he barked.

"My sister and I have come to deliver Dame Spencer's dogs," Max said, thinking on his feet. He pointed at the two terriers beside Kensy.

"Yes, of course." The fellow nodded, and Max dashed inside.

"What are you doing here?" he whispered to Kensy, who looked up at him in surprise. "And why didn't you tell me? I would have come with you."

Kensy shrugged. "I saw an opportunity and took it. Song was never going to bring us, and I guessed Wellie and Mac would know the way. It was lucky I brought them too. The man out front was so excited to see them and let me in without so much as a question."

"Is Dame Spencer here?" Max asked, sitting down beside her.

"The receptionist didn't say, but I assume so," the girl replied. "She told me to wait here."

Kensy and Max watched as a steady stream of employees entered the building and swiped themselves through a security screen that peeled back as their cards were accepted. The place was a hive of activity despite the fact it was almost the end of the workday. There were couriers dropping off deliveries and people waiting for appointments. Once, the receptionist reluctantly handed a pass to someone who had left their swipe card in their office. She gave them strict instructions to return it promptly.

Wellie and Mac sat at the children's feet, their tails thudding in anticipation.

"I know, I'm hungry too," Max said to the terriers. His stomach was grumbling and the thought of Song's homemade scones was only making things worse.

The receptionist hopped up and walked through a door behind her desk. For a building that minutes ago had been heaving with people, it was practically empty now. Max picked up a copy of the day's newspaper from the coffee table next to them and flicked through it. There was an article about rising power prices and another about the prime minister, who had upset an elderly pensioner by yelling at her in a supermarket parking lot, apparently fueled by a fit of road rage – just the usual stuff that made the daily news. Max turned to the section on world affairs and scoured it for any mention of the rebel uprising in Africa but found nothing.

Kensy's eyes were everywhere. She flinched as she watched the guard at the front door dig out a wad of earwax, which he then examined as if it were a nugget of gold. She saw a delivery driver earn the ire of the receptionist when he rushed in and dropped the parcel he was carrying so heavily on the counter it sounded as if whatever was inside was now in a thousand pieces. But it was something – or rather someone – behind the security screen that really seized the girl's attention.

"Max," she hissed, thumping her brother on the leg.

"Ow!" He closed the newspaper and glared at her. "What did you do that for?"

"I just saw Fitz," Kensy said, her mind reeling at what this could possibly mean. Fitz was meant to be in Africa, looking for their parents. "Through there, on the other side of the security screen."

Max looked at her the way he always did when she had a theory. "You must have seen someone who *looked* like Fitz, Kens."

"It was him. I know it was," she insisted. The girl marched to the security screen and stood on her tiptoes, craning her neck in an effort to see around it.

Her brother gathered up the dog leads and joined her. Wellie and Mac danced about, wagging their tails. Unable to see a thing, Kensy turned around and pouted. It was perfect timing, really, because at that moment the disgruntled receptionist took up the broken parcel and disappeared through a side door.

"Come on," Kensy said, running over to the reception desk.

Max glanced about nervously as his sister jumped onto the desk and snatched up the pass she'd seen the woman return only a minute before. Kensy swiped the card and dashed through the checkpoint toward the elevators. Without a second thought, Max and the dogs hurried after her.

Meanwhile, back at thirteen Ponsonby Terrace, Song's favorite country tune had come to its mournful end and he was suddenly aware of how eerily quiet the town house was. Master Maxim was taking an awfully long time to fetch his pullover. Come to think of it, Wellington and Mackintosh had not appeared for their dinner and Miss Kensington was absent too.

Song took a deep breath as the realization set in. He grabbed his coat and pulled it over his shoulders. "Confucius says those twins are far too clever for their own good," he declared, and raced upstairs and out the front door.

CHAPTER 22

AXJB PMBKZBO

Kensy pushed the elevator button and prayed they weren't about to meet anyone. To the twins' great relief, the doors opened to reveal an empty car.

"I don't know where you think we're going," Max grumbled, following her into the elevator. "If it was Fitz, we have no idea where he went and this building isn't exactly small. There are thirteen stories."

"It *was* Fitz. I'd know that bald head any-where." Kensy swiped the pass and pressed the button to take them to the top floor. "And I'm not leaving until I see Dame Spencer. Shouldn't we do everything we can to find Mum and Dad?"

The doors slid back and the two terriers scuttled into a dimly lit hall. There was a black-and-white marble floor and wood paneling lined with portraits of men from another time. Each was illuminated by a brass picture light, which reminded Kensy of the paintings on the stairwell at Alexandria, although some were a touch more modern. It wasn't until they reached the last one that Max stopped.

"Kens," he whispered, pointing to the brass plaque beneath it.

The man in the picture was handsome with a thick head of salt-and-pepper hair and clear blue eyes. Apart from a small dimple in his left cheek, he could have been . . .

Sharp footsteps in the hallway interrupted his thoughts and both children spun around to find Song coming toward them. He had swapped his usual black dinner jacket for a tailcoat and white tie. Wellie and Mac skittered behind Max's legs and began to growl, baring their teeth.

"Good afternoon, Master Maxim, Miss

Kensington," the butler said with a deep bow. "I am – Aaaachooooo!" An almighty sneeze cut the man short, and was followed by another three in quick succession. He removed a handkerchief from his pocket and blew his nose. "Please excuse me. I am dreadfully allergic to canines."

Max's eyebrows jumped. "You're Dame Spencer's city butler."

"Quite right, Master Maxim. I am Sidney," the man sniffled. "At your service."

Kensy's eyes widened. "Song didn't tell us you were twins!" she blurted. It was strange that he left that bit out.

Sidney nodded. "Song is my younger brother by a minute and a half."

Kensy grinned. "Max is younger than me by half an hour," she boasted.

"And she never lets me forget it," Max said, rolling his eyes.

The butler chortled with understanding. "Well, Confucius says –"

"Oh, don't tell me you like country music too?" Kensy said, recoiling.

"No, Miss Kensington. That is ghastly stuff."

Sidney shook his head vehemently. "I am a big fan of the King."

Kensy turned to her brother. "Does he mean Elvis Presley?"

Sidney swiveled his hips and spun his left arm like a flywheel. "Thank you, thank you very much," he boomed in a deep voice.

Kensy and Max stuffed their fists into their mouths to stop themselves from laughing as they followed their private Elvis impersonator to the end of the corridor. It was only when a female voice beckoned them to enter that Kensy began to feel slightly queasy. She found herself questioning if this had been a good idea after all.

The butler led them into a beautifully decorated office with a vast mahogany desk and matching bookshelves behind it. There was a black marble fireplace and several comfortable-looking couches. A colorful rug sat beneath them in the middle of the polished wood floor. "Ma'am, I would like to introduce Master Maxim Grey and his sister, Miss Kensington Grey," the man said, bowing, before retreating from the room.

Max gulped, remembering how his father often warned them to be careful of what they wished for.

Dame Spencer stood up from behind her desk. She was dressed in a striking navy pantsuit, her soft gray hair framing an older but still very attractive face. Her piercing green eyes reminded Max of someone, but he couldn't place it.

"Hello, children, it's lovely to meet you," she said. Her voice was clipped and perfunctory, as if she had a million other things she would rather be doing. "I see you've brought the dogs."

Max didn't know whether to let them go or to hold on more tightly, and Dame Spencer didn't help him with the decision either.

"We didn't mean to interrupt your work," Kensy began. "We just wanted to meet you and thank you for your wonderful hospitality . . . in person."

Max nodded. "Yes, thank you," he echoed. "I love your library at Alexandria. It's amazing, especially with all those first editions. And the automaton Song showed us is incredible. We'd never seen anything like that before."

Cordelia's lips began to curve into a smile but stopped halfway.

Kensy nudged her brother to continue.

Max looked at her and frowned. He didn't see why it was up to him to speak, seeing as though it was Kensy who got them into this mess in the first place. "As soon as Fitz brings our parents back, we'll be off to Zermatt for the winter, but perhaps we might visit you again one day," he said lamely.

"For goodness' sake, Max," Kensy sighed. She turned to the woman. "We don't want to visit you again," she said plainly. "No offense. We were just wondering whether you had reporters in Africa who might be able to help track down our parents. We wouldn't expect you to help us for free. Max and I have been saving up our birthday money for years and we hardly ever touch our bank accounts. Or maybe you could run a story about Mum and Dad and then more people will be on the lookout? They're probably not the only aid workers missing . . ."

Dame Spencer remained stone-faced as the girl prattled on, her lips pressed tightly in a straight line.

Kensy was about to start up again when her brother touched her arm. "We're really sorry to have bothered you, Dame Spencer," the boy said. "We should head home – to your home – and I think Wellie might have to go out."

All eyes turned to the pup dancing about in circles.

"Oh, he just wants a cuddle." Dame Spencer walked around her desk and bent down to pick up the dog, cradling him in her arms. Wellie rewarded her with a tongue to the cheek. "I'm sorry, children, but you've caught me at an impossible time. I will see what I can do to help locate your parents, but I can't promise anything."

There was a loud knock on the door before Song poked his head in. To say he looked sheepish was something of an understatement. "My apologies, ma'am. I . . ."

Cordelia silenced him with a hand. She

set Wellie down on the floor and gave Mac a ruffle on the head before walking back around to the other side of her desk. "Thank you for coming to see me," she said. "Make sure you look after them, Song, and perhaps you could keep a closer eye on things in future."

Song bowed and, blushing, guided the children and dogs out the door.

The twins looked at one another, their faces etched with disappointment. Dame Spencer might have been a lot of things, but helpful wasn't one of them.

CHAPTER 23

PEXALTP

Contrary to expectations, Kensy and Max left the *Beacon* with more questions than when they'd arrived. They were also waiting for Song to tell them off for going to see Dame Spencer, but he was strangely silent on the subject.

"Why didn't you tell us you were a twin?" Kensy asked as they walked home. She was holding Mac's lead, and Max was in charge of Wellie's. "You and Sidney are so alike. For a minute there we thought it was you in the hall."

"My brother is at least half an inch shorter than me and he has the worst taste in music,"

Song replied somewhat testily. He peered at the girl out of the corner of his eye. "Sidney is still a good person but not nearly as good-looking."

"*He* has terrible taste in music?" Kensy began, receiving a swift smack to the arm from Max.

The children turned left past The White Swan. Although carrying on down the main road would have been a more direct route, Song was happy for the dogs to lead the way. They were clearly trying to avoid the crowds and doing a fine job of it as there was barely a soul on the side street.

Song was right behind them when his phone buzzed inside his pocket. He pulled it out and looked at the caller ID. "Oh," he said with a grimace. "Sorry, children, it's the boss. I must answer." He put the phone to his ear, but from the look on the man's face, Dame Spencer wasn't calling to congratulate him on his child-minding skills. "Yes, ma'am, I will be more careful in future," he said. "I do apologize."

"Way to go getting Song into trouble, Kens," Max said, nudging his sister. He quickened his pace so as not to listen in on the man's private conversation and gestured for Song to meet them around the corner. The butler nodded, then flinched and moved the phone away from his ear. "We need to apologize to him when we get home," Max said to Kensy. "You shouldn't have run off like that."

"Okay, okay, I'm sorry," Kensy said. "I didn't think. But if we hadn't gone, we wouldn't have seen Fitz. Should we tell Master Confusing about that too?"

"Are you really sure it was him?" Max said. "Like, *really* sure and not one of your conspiracy theories?"

Kensy gritted her teeth in frustration. "I know what I saw, Max. Fitz has been looking after us since we were babies. He's like our second dad. Of course it was him and I want to know why he lied to us."

Max gulped. He wanted to know that too. "What did you make of Dame Spencer?"

"Well, I don't think she was very happy to meet us – and I don't believe her when she said that she'd do anything about Mum and Dad. She seemed pretty standoffish, if you ask me,"

Kensy replied. "Maybe she's miserable because of all the bad things that have happened to her, like Mrs. Grigsby said."

Suddenly, two men dressed head to toe in black, and with balaclavas covering their faces, dashed out of an alleyway and lunged at the children.

"Kensy, look out!" Max called, as he ducked under one fellow's muscular arms.

Wellie latched on to the man's pants. The dog pulled and growled, and was at one point lifted off the ground, but refused to let go. The other man grabbed Kensy around the middle. She smacked his head and tried to pull off his balaclava. Then she remembered what Fitz had taught her about self-defense and jammed her fingers into his neck, aiming for a pressure point. The fellow howled in pain and released her. Kensy kicked him as hard as she could in the shin, while Mac latched on to his worn leather boot.

The other goon struck Wellie hard under the rib cage, launching the little dog into the air. Wellie yelped in pain and tumbled backward over and over. Max ran at the man and crash tackled him to the ground.

"Hey, what do you think you're doing? Stop that!" a girl shouted.

Kensy was stunned to see Autumn sprinting toward them with Carlos close behind. Autumn scissor kicked Kensy's attacker in the nose. Carlos, meanwhile, ran to help Max, who was now pinned to the ground. Carlos shoved the man as hard as he could, sending him crashing onto his side. Max managed to get a grip on the balaclava but couldn't hold on. The thug jumped to his feet and flung Carlos away like a rag doll, then lashed out at Max, who made another attempt to unmask him. This time Max spun around, using his legs like a sweeper. He connected with the man's ankles and the fellow collapsed onto the pavement. The boy jumped on him and sat astride his chest while Carlos tried to get hold of the man's flailing arms.

To their right, Autumn and Kensy circled their attacker, who was down on all fours, his nose dripping blood onto the sidewalk.

He hobbled to his feet and fiddled with an earpiece that had fallen out.

Max made one last grab at his assailant. He tore the balaclava at the side a little, revealing some of the top half of the man's face. For just a second the boy looked into a pair of watery blue eyes. The roar of an engine and screech of brakes diverted Max's attention as a black van pulled up beside them. The sliding door opened and the pair of brutes broke free and leapt into the vehicle. It hurtled away, disappearing around a bend in the road. The one positive was that Max had managed to commit the number plate to memory.

Kensy was doubled over, trying to catch her breath. Autumn offered her a hand and the two girls embraced tightly. "I don't know how you happened to be here, but thanks," Kensy wheezed.

Max patted Carlos on the back just as Song rounded the corner. The man was stunned by the scene before him. His eyes found Wellington, who had a piece of one of the fellow's trousers hanging from his mouth, then the children.

"What has happened?" he gasped, rushing over to them.

"Some guys just tried to kidnap us," Max puffed. "Maybe it had something do with your unexpected visitor yesterday."

Song clutched at his head. "Oh my goodness, I should have been with you. I am so sorry."

"Why would anyone want to hurt us?" Kensy could feel tears stinging her eyes but was determined not to cry – especially not in front of Autumn and Carlos.

Song was at a loss for words. He shook his head at the ground. "I do not know. Perhaps it was a case of mistaken identity. Most importantly, are you hurt?" Song assessed each of the children for visible injuries, then gathered the dogs' leads. "We must return home."

"Shouldn't we call the police?" Max said.

Carlos and Autumn exchanged glances, then looked at Song.

"No, I will report it as soon as we are safely inside," Song said firmly. "It will take hours for the constabulary to come and by then it will be even colder and you will be hungrier.

Your friends need to get home too. If we call now, they must stay to be witnesses. I will arrange for them to give their statements."

Kensy shivered. A stiff breeze had sprung up and she could feel the chill against her cheeks.

Autumn gave her another hug. "You'll be okay," she said.

Kensy brushed at her eyes. "Thanks. If it wasn't for you two . . . I hate to think what could have happened."

Carlos shook Max's hand. "You should come to my kung fu class. You're a natural."

Max grinned and rubbed his neck. He was kind of proud of himself for having fought off his attacker. All those years of sparring with Fitz in the gym must have helped. And Kensy had held her own too.

"Miss Autumn, Master Carlos, do you need assistance in getting home? I can call you a cab," Song offered.

"No, I'm not far," Autumn said, and peeked at her watch. "Oh gosh, look at the time. My aunt will be wondering where I've got to. I'll see you tomorrow."

And with that the girl turned and hurried back toward the main road.

Carlos gave a wave. "See you at school," the boy said, and scurried away in the same direction the van had gone.

Kensy glimpsed a curtain in one of the terraces pull back and then drop down again.

How was it that two kids could be attacked at peak hour on the streets of London and, right when it happens, there is no one around, Kensy thought to herself. And then there was Carlos and Autumn. She couldn't help but notice how calm her friends had been in the face of danger, as if things like that happened all the time.

Song guided the children along the dark streets back to number thirteen. He hesitated at the door.

"Are you expecting someone?" Max asked.

The butler turned the key in the lock and the group walked inside. "I most certainly hope not," he replied.

CHAPTER 24

X JBPPXDB

Max was still half asleep when he realized that his wrist was buzzing. He was having a spectacularly wonderful dream about his parents and Kensy and Fitz. They were all skiing together in Thredbo and he'd just beaten Kensy down the mountain for a third time. Max forced himself back to sleep – he wasn't ready to leave them yet – when his watch buzzed again. It was the same annoying pattern . . .

His eyes flew open. Could it be? Max threw off the covers and shot into his sister's bedroom, picking a path through the clothes that were strewn across the floor.

"Kensy!" he whispered loudly, shaking her by the shoulders. "Is your watch vibrating?"

His sister sat bolt upright. "So now you believe me," she said, and reached over to pick hers up from the bedside cabinet. She held on to it and waited, but there was nothing.

Max sat down beside her. He reached out and placed her hand over his wrist and the pattern replayed again.

Kensy looked at him. "Is that Morse code?" she asked, her eyes wide.

Max nodded.

"Quick, write it down! You're better at it than I am." The girl could barely contain herself, and thrust a pencil and the notepad on her bedside table into his hands.

Max darted over to her desk and waited for the cycle to start again. There were a lot of short shakes and staccato buzzes, but he managed to catch it all. Morse code was something Fitz had taught them – it was tricky at first, but after lots of practice Max had proved to be especially good at it.

Kensy watched as her brother transcribed

the dots and lines. "Well, what does it say?" she demanded impatiently.

"Alive," Max read aloud. "Tell no one. Trust only Fitz. Love M and D."

Kensy gasped and hugged her brother. "I knew it! I just knew it! What do we do now? We have to tell Song!"

"No, Kens. Mum and Dad expressly said to tell no one and to only trust Fitz," Max cautioned. "And if you really did spot Fitz at the *Beacon* offices yesterday, I'm not even sure we can trust *him*."

"Don't remind me about yesterday," Kensy said with a sigh. "I hardly slept last night. I kept thinking someone was going to come through the window and grab me." The girl shuddered involuntarily.

When they'd returned home the previous evening, Song had made a call and just after dinner two plainclothes detectives arrived at the house. The children had given their statements and the officers said they'd be in touch, but considering their attackers had worn balaclavas and the number plate had been stolen, there was little chance of finding them. It seemed their attempted kidnapping was as much a mystery as everything else that had happened the past few days. The detective even tried to cast doubt on the idea that it was an attempted kidnapping, speculating that it might have been a robbery gone wrong. When Max pointed out that it was hardly likely that two schoolkids would have anything particularly valuable on them, the man had quickly closed his notebook and stood up to leave.

Kensy picked up the piece of paper Max had scribbled the code on. "What do you think? Do we tell Fitz about this when he turns up from whatever he's been doing?"

Max shrugged. "I'm not sure. We know Mum and Dad are alive and there has to be a reason they've told us not to say anything. I wish we could get a message back to them."

"That's a great idea! What if I try pulling my watch apart?" Kensy suggested. "I mean, even if I mess it up, we've still got yours and that's how we got the message anyway." She turned it over in her hand, trying to see how the back might come off, but there was no obvious panel. "I could ask Mrs. Vanden Boom to help me work out how to get into it. She has a pretty cool tool kit."

"She might get suspicious," Max said, biting his lip.

Kensy arched an eyebrow. "Of what? Stop being paranoid. If I tell her it's not working properly, I'm sure she'll help. She's a science teacher – a slightly strange one, I'll give you that, but I don't imagine she's working for MI6."

Max grinned. "Does anyone really work for MI6?" he said, thinking back to what Gary had told them.

Kensy pulled some clean underwear from her top drawer and hurried into the en suite bathroom, then poked her head back around the door. "Don't just stand there, Max. We've got to get to school early and find Mrs. Vanden Boom!"

CHAPTER 25

YBFKD KBFDEYLOIV

Song peered up and down the street, tapping his foot impatiently. The three of them were standing outside the town house, waiting for their taxi.

"We can walk," Kensy grumbled, although there was a small part of her that liked the idea of not being on the street after what had happened the previous afternoon and her near miss with the cab the day before.

"That is out of the question. The policemen recommended I deliver you door-to-door, so that is what I intend to do," Song replied.

"Mr. Fitz has left you in my care and I would never forgive myself if anything happened to you."

The door to number fourteen across the road opened and Derek Grigsby walked out. His eyes were red rimmed and his gangster clothes looked as if they were covered in dust. Max wondered what sort of job he was doing for Mrs. Brightside. She must have been having a lot of renovations done.

"I'll be back later, Esme. I gotta look after the shop for me mam this mornin'," the young man called, pulling the door shut. He looked up and noticed Song and the children on the steps. "Mornin'," he said with a wave.

Song waved back. "Good morning, Derek."

"You waitin' for someone?" Derek asked, crossing the road to his car.

"A taxi to go to school, as silly as that sounds," Kensy said. She checked her watch. They could have been there by now.

Derek looked confused. "Don't you just go to Central London Free? Is there somefin' wrong wiv your legs?"

Kensy and Max shook their heads. "Song wants us to get a lift this morning – he's a bit overprotective," the boy explained. "I'm Max, by the way, and this is my sister, Kensy."

The butler had just dialed the number to find out where their tardy driver was.

"I can take you," Derek offered. "I have to go that way to get rid of some stuff in me trunk."

Song's ears pricked up. "No!" he shouted, then calmed himself. "I am sure that our vehicle is not far away." The butler went back to tapping his foot impatiently as he waited for someone to answer his call.

Max glanced at his watch. It was getting late. If they wanted to see Mrs. Vanden Boom, they had to get to school before the bell. "I think Derek's okay, you know," he whispered to his sister, who had looked a little uncertain about the offer. After everything Kensy had been through in the past few days, it was understandable that she was wary.

"Well, are you comin'?" Derek asked.

Song jiggled on the spot and beckoned the children over to him. They huddled together like a football team having a pep talk. "Derek is an idiot," Song said quietly. He flashed an overly enthusiastic grin at the young man, who was standing outside the open driver's door. He hoped the idiot hadn't heard him.

"Please, Song, we really do need to get to school," Kensy begged. "It's important."

"I promise I'll drive slow, Song – you can pay me back by makin' those dumplins for me old lady," Derek said with a wink. "She won't be round for much longer, so you'd better 'op to it. And I would much prefer to 'ave 'er in a better mood. She's been snappin' my 'ead off every day these past few weeks."

"It is very kind of you to offer, but I would rather we wait for the cab," Song said, turning toward the other end of the street.

The twins looked at one another and nodded.

"Sorry, Song, I don't know why you can't just get another taxi – it's not as if there aren't a gazillion of them around here, but your guy is late and we have to go," Max said, as the twins clambered into Derek's blingy hatchback.

Song rushed toward the car and tried to pull the door open, but it was stuck. "Miss Kensington, I really must insist. You and your brother will get out of that vehicle immediately."

Kensy put down the window. "We'll be fine."

Before the butler had time to say another word, Derek had fired up the sputtery engine and pulled out into the roadway. The children gave a wave just as a taxi turned off the main road into Ponsonby Terrace. True to his word, Derek drove very carefully indeed. He used his indicators and kept well below the speed limit.

The twins soon found out that he was quite the talker too, firing questions at them about school and what they liked to do in their spare time and how long they were staying at Song's house. Fortunately, the children were as good at evading them as he was at asking. It turned out that Derek used to love school because it meant six hours away from his mum.

"Is your mum moving?" Kensy asked. After his earlier comment about the woman not being around much longer, she was keen to know why.

"Who'd want to live in England if you could be in the Caribbean, eh?" Derek smirked, revealing a gold front tooth that Kensy hadn't noticed before. She wondered if it was real.

"Has she sold the shop?" Max asked.

Suddenly, Derek the talker didn't know what to say. "Um, uh, yeah, somefin' like that." He pulled up at the school gates. "Looks like a prison, don't it? It's not, though. The teachers here never leave, you know. I reckon it must be the best school in the whole of London, probably in the whole world – even if some of the staff are a bit weird. Mr. MacGregor has been here forever."

"That's good to know," Kensy said. Derek might not have been the brightest star in the sky, despite his sparkly car and earring, but he seemed to have a kind heart. He was doing all those jobs for Mrs. Brightside and he helped his mum in the shop too. The girl felt a twinge of guilt for having laughed at him the other night when Song and Gary had been telling stories.

The children piled out of the car and thanked Derek for the lift.

Max looked up to see a taxi drive past with Song in the back seat. "Someone couldn't help himself," he murmured, and he and Kensy both gave the butler a wave and a smile.

Song grinned sheepishly and waved back.

CHAPTER 26

TXQZE LRQ

The twins dumped their bags in their lockers and headed for the science room. Although they were earlier than usual, there were still plenty of students and teachers about. Max knocked on the door of the lab and poked his head around.

"Hello? Mrs. Vanden Boom, are you here?" he called, as the pair walked inside.

They were just about to leave when Kensy spun around. "Did you hear that?"

A muffled noise seemed to be coming from the cupboard at the back. Max turned the handle and pulled the door open. The children were stunned to see Romilly Vanden Boom stumble out of the dark space.

"Oh, thank heavens you two came along." The woman grabbed hold of the nearest bench in an effort to regain her balance. She pushed a loose strand of curls away from her face and straightened her lab coat. "I'm running frightfully late."

"What were you doing in there?" Kensy asked, peering inside what appeared to be a supply store.

"I've told Magoo for years that we need to get a closer on that door. Once the silly thing shuts, it's impossible to pick the lock from the inside. It's not the first time I've been stuck and it won't be the last, but I'm very glad you two found me. I'd never have gotten all my prep work done before class," the woman said. She looked expectantly at the children. "Now, I presume you didn't just come to rescue me?"

"I was hoping you might be able to help me with my watch," Kensy said, removing the timepiece and handing it to the woman.

"I think it's the battery and you have all those fancy tools. I didn't want to bother going to a jeweler if I could fix it myself."

The science teacher smiled. "Well, I can give you a minute – think of it as repayment for springing me from the cupboard."

Kensy and Max followed her to the long lab bench at the front of the room.

Mrs. Vanden Boom turned the watch over in her hand and studied the back, then picked up a large magnifying glass. "Impossible," she muttered. "This looks just like an MK 13."

Kensy and Max wondered what she meant. There were a lot more mmms and ahhs, but the teacher didn't say anything else for quite some time.

"Can you see what I need to do with it?" Kensy asked.

The woman shook her head. "It's the most curious thing. Where did you get it?"

Kensy looked at her brother. Perhaps this hadn't been the best idea. Mrs. Vanden Boom was still scrutinizing the timepiece intensely. Max pulled his cuff down over his own watch.

"For my birthday," the girl said. "It was a present. I think it must have come from Australia."

"Would I be able to hold on to it for a little while?" the teacher asked. "I'm intrigued."

Kensy hadn't anticipated that. The reality of being separated from the one thing that linked her to her missing parents filled her with dread.

Mrs. Vanden Boom didn't look up. "I promise not to lose it." She was completely absorbed by the device.

"That's a great idea, Mrs. Vanden Boom," Max said, earning a glare from his sister. "We'll come back at lunchtime, if that's okay."

The bell rang loudly, signifying the start of lessons.

"*Is* that okay?" Kensy repeated angrily.

Romilly glanced up. "What, dear?"

"Can we come and see you at lunch?" the girl asked.

"Oh no, not today," the woman said. "I've got a meeting, then science club and I can't tell you what else. Come by tomorrow before you head home, although I might need it over the weekend." She opened a drawer and retrieved the tiniest screwdriver Kensy had ever seen. "Off you go. You don't want to be late for class, now, do you?"

Max practically had to drag his sister from the room.

"Why did you do that?" Kensy fumed the second they stepped into the hall outside.

"We've still got mine," Max reasoned, trying to calm her down. "You said yourself it was a bonus to have two watches and that's why we could try to get into yours."

"You shouldn't have let her have it. I don't trust her," Kensy said in a wobbly voice. "Have you forgotten what Mum and Dad said? Trust Fitz and no one else – that includes teachers! Sometimes you're so . . ." Kensy paused, as if searching for the right word. "Infuriating!" She stormed toward the lockers, which were a hive of activity.

Carlos had just put his things away and closed the door when Kensy walked past. "Hi, how are you feeling?" he asked the girl.

"Fine," Kensy snapped, and continued walking.

Carlos frowned. "Was it something I said?"

Max shook his head. "No, something I did. Why don't you have any books?"

"We're going to the Tate Gallery for a lecture this morning," the lad replied. "Can't guarantee it'll be very exciting, though."

Kensy opened her locker and pulled out her art folder. She closed the door and glanced around to see if Autumn or Harper were about.

"Looking for your besties?" Lola smirked. "They left without you."

"Yeah, they left without you," Misha parroted, hovering an inch behind her friend.

Kensy took a deep breath and tried to control her temper. "Pipe down, Lola. And seriously, Misha, you should learn to speak for yourself." Kensy caught sight of Carlos and her brother standing by their lockers empty-handed. "Where's your stuff for art?" she called, still angry with her brother about the watch.

"We're going to the Tate Gallery," Max said.

"You don't need to bring anything."

"We're meeting Mr. Frizzle at the front door," Carlos added. "But make sure you pronounce it like 'gazelle,' not 'swizzle' – he gets annoyed otherwise."

Kensy huffed and opened her locker, which promptly disgorged its entire contents all over the floor.

"Do you need some help with that?" Lola asked sweetly.

Kensy looked up at her, softening a little. "Really?"

"No!" Lola sneered. She batted her eyelashes, which looked like they belonged on a jersey cow. "Not my problem."

"Yeah, not my problem," Misha echoed, grinning, and the two flounced away.

"Urgh!" Kensy took another deep breath. "Seriously, could those two be any more horrible?" she muttered, and began to pick up her detritus.

An older girl who was passing by stopped and knelt down to help. "Are they giving you a hard time?" she asked, gesturing over Kensy's shoulder at Lola and Misha.

"It's okay. I can handle them," Kensy said, jutting out her chin. "They're not the meanest kids I've ever encountered, but they could just about be the most brainless."

The girl laughed. She had long dark hair tied up in a ponytail and a dimple in the middle of her left cheek. "I'm Amelie Jagger," she said, handing Kensy the last of her books.

"Kensy Grey. And . . . thanks," she said, her eyes watering.

"Are you okay?" Amelie asked, a crease forming on her brow.

Kensy nodded and smiled. "Yeah, it's just been a bit of a rough week."

"You mean your parents," Amelie said. Not a second after the last word left her lips, the girl's hand flew to her mouth.

Kensy frowned. "What about my parents?" she whispered, taking a step toward the girl. "Do you know something? You do, don't you?"

Amelie's eyes darted around the hall. "No, sorry," she said, shaking her head and backing away. "I-I was thinking of someone else. A girl called Stella looks a lot like you. I, um, heard her parents were in a car accident – I was confused. Sorry. It was lovely to meet you, but I better get to class."

Kensy watched as Amelie scurried away. She wasn't buying it. The girl was acting as though she was expecting a hand to reach out of the ceiling and grab her. Kensy closed her locker and hurried to reception with Amelie's words ringing in her ears. She was absolutely certain neither she nor Max had breathed a word about their missing parents to anyone.

CHAPTER 27

QEB QXQB

Elliot Frizzle greeted the class in the reception area, quickly checking off their names and explaining that they were going to be hearing from world-renowned art critic Hugo Kellogg. None of the children had ever heard of him, but the teacher assured them that their guest speaker knew his stuff and, despite some protests that it would be boring, Mr. Frizzle guaranteed they'd enjoy themselves.

"Do we get our money back if we don't, sir?" Sachin asked.

"Considering it's a free lecture, I'd say that's a no," the teacher replied.

"Can we have our time back then?" the boy persisted, earning himself a hairy eyeball.

"That's another no from me." Mr. Frizzle turned to his two new students and beamed. His clothing was as bright as his smile and it made sense that he taught art and design. While most people couldn't have gotten away with the clash of red and purple, on Mr. Frizzle it worked. "Hello, Maxim, Kensington, it's lovely to meet you both. I trust that you're settling in and enjoying our little piece of paradise here in London."

"Yes, sir," Max replied with a grin. Kensy could only manage a stiff smile.

The headmaster walked out of his office. "Enjoy your outing, children," he boomed. "I look forward to hearing all about it, and if anyone decides that it's not worth paying attention, I'll have you know I am in need of a new attendant for Kevin." He looked over at Mrs. Potts. "How is Charlie's finger? Does he still have it?"

"He's kidding, right?" Max whispered.

Carlos grimaced. "Probably not."

"Poor lad had a nasty infection. Turned gangrenous, I believe," Mr. MacGregor added with a chuckle, before striding back into his office and closing the door.

"Seriously, he's a nutter," Dante said, as the children headed outside. The lad turned and saw their headmaster grinning like a Cheshire cat from his office window.

"He just loves playing tricks, that's all." Harper smiled and gave the man a wave. "You know he's completely harmless."

The children split into pairs and followed Mr. Frizzle along the sidewalk and down the street. They walked through Millbank Gardens and across another street to the Clore Learning Center, which was the entrance used by schools for visits to the Tate Gallery.

Autumn fell into step beside Kensy. She leaned in and bumped her head against the girl's shoulder. "You okay?"

Kensy was still raging inside about Max leaving her watch with Mrs. Vanden Boom, but that wasn't Autumn's problem. She stifled a yawn. "Yes, thanks to you. Although I didn't sleep very well. I kept thinking those guys were going to work out where we lived and come back for us. Did the police take your statement last night?"

Autumn nodded but didn't elaborate.

"It's hard to imagine this was the Millbank prison site," Max said, as they entered the grand old building. He marveled at the soaring ceilings and marble columns. "Bet that was a bit different."

"We studied it in history class earlier this year," Carlos said. "Apparently, it was a dreadful place – freezing cold, horrible food, ten to a cell. Then again, my dad says that's what his boarding school was like and I should count myself lucky he had no desire to continue the family tradition."

Mr. Frizzle guided the children to a tiered lecture theatre, where they waited for their guest speaker to arrive. The children chatted, but after almost fifteen minutes, the group was getting restless. A couple of the boys made paper planes, which they launched just as a young woman poked her head into the room and indicated that she needed to speak to their teacher. Fortunately, none of them made contact, whizzing past her head instead.

After several minutes of hushed conversation punctuated by the odd "Oh no!" and "Heavens be!" from Mr. Frizzle, the man walked down the stairs to the front of the room, dodging another couple of missiles launched from the back row.

"Something's up," Autumn said, eyeing the teacher. "He always fiddles with his bow tie when he's nervous."

Mr. Frizzle cleared his throat. "Children, I am terribly sorry to inform you that Mr. Kellogg has come down with a case of influenza gifted to him by his son, Milo, whose kindergarten is currently in the grip of a pandemic," the man explained.

Dante raised his hand. "Do you know what his temperature is, sir?"

There was a titter of giggles from the class.

Mr. Frizzle rolled his eyes. "And why would I know that level of detail? Varma, don't go asking me what color pajamas the man is wearing because I'm not aware of that either."

The children burst out laughing.

"All right, that is quite enough. Perhaps I'll just take you back to school and we can do yard duty for the rest of the double period," the man threatened. Silence descended upon the room immediately. "Yes, I thought that might not be a popular choice. Now, we have generously been granted access to a brand-new exhibition, which I think you will find quite fascinating. As most of you know, the Tate Gallery is curator of British artworks for the entire country and that is not only limited to paintings. The exhibit will officially be opened this evening by the mayor of London and we've been given a sneak peek, along with some members of the Friends of the Gallery."

"What is it, sir?" Roderick, a mouse of a boy, squeaked.

Elliot Frizzle adjusted his right cuff link and smoothed the lapels on his purple blazer. Max couldn't help thinking that, with his mop of wild blond curls and colorful clothes, the man resembled Willy Wonka from the old film he and Kensy had watched a while back. "An exhibition of Laurence Graff's work, one of Britain's finest jewelers. I've been told that the collection would rival that of the crown jewels, and considering you are going to be spending a month or so creating a jeweled work of your own next term, the timing couldn't be better."

"At least we don't have to go back to school early," Carlos said. There was a murmur of agreement from the other students.

The children filed out of the lecture theatre and followed their guide called Claire through to a long gallery at the front of the building. She delivered a brief introduction that canvassed the jeweler's humble beginnings as an apprentice in London, to his traveling the globe outfitting the rich, royal and famous. The exhibition, Claire told the class, comprised some of Laurence Graff's most valuable pieces, including the extraordinary Peacock Brooch. The children craned their necks to catch a glimpse of the magnificent jewel, which was reported to be worth a staggering eighty million pounds.

Carlos let out a low whistle. "Whoa, that would buy a few holidays."

"I think you could probably buy yourself an island or two for that amount of money," Max said, grinning.

"I'd get a jet," Sachin said. "So that I could

fly all over the world and watch every single cricket match – especially when England plays Australia for the Ashes – and maybe finance a Bollywood movie and star in it too."

The class giggled. Sachin was a cricket tragic who prided himself on being a total cliché. His parents ran a curry house in Brick Lane and he adored everything to do with Bollywood. He often poked fun at himself for being the quintessential subcontinental Englishman.

Carlos turned to Max. "What would you do with that much money?"

"Buy a house and stay in the same place for a while," the lad said. He caught sight of the look on his sister's face and wished he hadn't said anything.

Kensy, Autumn and Harper wandered over to admire a pair of dazzling tiaras. One was lavished with emeralds and sapphires, and the other had yellow and white diamonds. They were both breathtaking.

While the girls lingered at the neighboring display of earrings, Kensy went in search of something more exciting. She'd heard Claire mention a jewel-encrusted scimitar to Mr.

Frizzle. As she rounded the side of a long row of cabinets, she spotted Esme Brightside hunched over the Peacock Brooch exhibit and came to a skidding stop. She decided to wait until the old woman moved on before taking a look at the scimitar beside it.

It was then that Kensy noticed an attendant in an orange-and-black uniform standing in the corner of the room. She looked vaguely familiar and seemed to be watching Mrs. Brightside very closely. That's when Kensy realized she was the third woman in the huddle of grannies she and Max had seen a couple of times, including outside Mrs. Grigsby's shop.

Suddenly, a high-pitched alarm sounded. Everyone winced and covered their ears, turning this way and that trying to work out what was going on. Kensy couldn't help but feel a little disappointed that she probably wasn't going to get a look at the scimitar after all.

"Keep calm, children, there is no need to panic," Claire instructed, while Mr. Frizzle buzzed around the room like a mosquito.

"Be sensible, everyone," he urged, blatantly

disregarding his own advice.

Kensy saw Esme Brightside shake her head and roll her eyes, as if the whole thing was the most dreadful inconvenience.

The lights flickered on and off until – *boomph!* – they went out completely. Even in the near darkness, Kensy didn't miss it. The woman in the uniform strode purposefully toward Mrs. Brightside, who moved her arm ever so slightly, leaving the top of her enormous bag open. The attendant had something in her hand except that right at that moment a young boy collided with the pair, sending Mrs. Brightside flying in one direction and the attendant in another.

"You naughty little toad!" Esme shouted after the lad.

When the lights were turned back on, Kensy noticed an envelope on the floor. It hadn't been there seconds ago and she wondered if the woman in uniform had dropped it. But she was gone now and Esme Brightside was hotfooting it to the nearest exit. In fact, the old woman was looking remarkably sprightly. Kensy scooped up the envelope and was about to go after the woman when Claire ushered the class in a different direction.

"This way, and hurry please," she said, an octave higher than before.

Kensy shoved it into her blazer pocket.

The alarm was still screaming and people were beginning to panic. There were mothers with young children in prams, and elderly folks in wheelchairs, as well as loads of tourists, some nonplussed and others nervous. Kensy turned and saw a young fellow trying to assist Esme Brightside, only to receive a solid whack from her walking stick. The old woman almost skipped down the stairs.

"She's such a fake," the girl muttered under her breath.

As they entered the main foyer, the smell of smoke filled the air and the sound of wailing sirens grew louder. The children jostled out of the side doors onto the street and Mr. Frizzle began to count heads. The fact that he had acquired an extra student caused some concern. He checked again to find that he'd managed to pick up a lad from a primary school in Croydon who was also on an excursion. The boy's poor teacher was beside herself on the forecourt at the front of the gallery.

Kensy pulled the envelope from her pocket and turned it over. On the front were the initials E. B., so she reasoned that it would belong to Mrs. Esme Brightside. The woman must have dropped it in the kerfuffle. Kensy would return it to her after school or, on second thoughts, maybe she'd convince Max to do it.

"What's that?" her brother asked, appearing at her side.

"I'm not sure." Kensy showed him the sealed packet and explained what she'd just witnessed. She resisted the urge to tear it open even though she desperately wanted to know what was inside. "I'll put it through the letter box this afternoon. I don't really want to talk to her."

By now Mr. Frizzle had returned the other boy to his very relieved teacher and rounded up his own students. "It looks as if they have things under control," the man reported. "Fire in a rubbish bin, apparently. Someone must have been having a sneaky cigarette and threw the butt into a bin."

Kensy glanced around and spotted a familiar figure. If he hadn't been dressed in a cheap ill-fitting suit with a dark shock of hair and a fedora hat at an impossible angle, she would have sworn it was Derek Grigsby. She nudged her brother. "Is that who I think it is?"

Max peered across the road. "It sort of looks like an older version of Derek. Why would he be here in disguise? Actually, why would he be here at all? This is the last place I would've thought he'd hang out."

"Maybe he's with Mrs. Brightside," Kensy said. "I saw her inside." She pulled the envelope out of her pocket again and felt around it to see if she could work out what was inside. It was really none of her concern, but the entire business was very odd. And why Derek Grigsby would be incognito at the gallery was anyone's guess. It didn't make sense at all. Then again, not much about Kensy and Max's lives did at the moment.

CHAPTER 28

QBIBMELKB

The children returned to school to find that a game of telephone about their miraculous escape from the gallery was gathering momentum at every turn. By lunchtime, things had gotten completely out of hand with rumors of an explosion and a hostage crisis doing the rounds. Mr. MacGregor decided to rein it in lest he be confronted with a group of anxious parents that afternoon.

The dining room thrummed with hungry students as the headmaster stood up from his seat at the teachers' table and walked to the microphone.

"Good afternoon, everyone," he boomed, silencing the clunking of cutlery and excitable chatter. He looked around at the teachers' table, where several of his colleagues were still speaking, and cleared his throat, waiting for his staff to fall into line. When the man was confident there was dead silence, he continued. "I would like to let you all know that while Mr. Frizzle's art class –" He stopped abruptly, taking account of the teacher glaring at him. "Sorry, I meant Mr. Friz-*elle's* art class. Did I get it right that time, Elliot?"

The teacher pursed his lips and nodded, wondering for the thousandth time if he might be better off changing the spelling of his name by deed poll. At least then there would be no excuses for mispronunciations.

Mr. MacGregor gave the man a nod and continued. "Yes, while Mr. Friz-*elle's* class was visiting the Tate this morning, there was a very small and inconsequential fire in a rubbish bin. All students were immediately evacuated and accounted for and, in fact, I hear that we almost picked up an extra."

"That's not what we heard, sir," Alfie called out. "From the rumors going around school, the whole place was burning to the ground and the kids just made it out by the skin of their teeth."

Mr. MacGregor looked at the lad pointedly. "Yes, Alfie, I'd heard that too and, given we can see the gallery from the front of the school, I'd say that was more than a slight exaggeration. Now, we really must nip nonsense like this in the bud. I can't abide such silliness and, if I find out who stoked the fire, pardon the pun, they'll be looking after Kevin for the rest of the term. And I can tell you he seems awfully hungry at the moment."

There was a collective gasp. No one wanted that job.

The headmaster was about to say something else when a loud shout came from the back of the room followed by the clanging of metal.

Magoo's shoulders slumped. "Oh, for goodness' sake," he muttered, rubbing his forehead.

The children turned to see two ancient

Roman soldiers barreling into the dining room, swords flailing and shouting at each other in Latin. Max recognized some of the words and giggled at his sister, who was sitting across from him and appeared to have recovered from her earlier bad mood.

"Who is that?" Kensy whispered to Autumn.

The girl smiled. "Just wait, you'll see."

The pair of soldiers parried and thrust down the center of the room. One of them spun around, swinging their sword with them, and missed the top of Alfie's curly hair by a whisker.

The girl sitting beside the lad pulled a thatch from the top of the boy's head and held it up. "You cut his hair!" she cried, garnering laughs from the rest of the students.

Magoo MacGregor was growing more impatient by the second. He was starving and patently aware that his lunch was getting cold. He'd asked Mrs. Trimm to give him extra gravy on his bangers and mash too, and had been looking forward to it all morning.

"Oh, for goodness' sake, Reffell, you've made

your point," the man barked. "I'm sure that the children are as excited about the history excursion as you are. Would you like to stop all this nonsense and come and tell them whatever it is you need to say this time?"

Monty Reffell and his partner, who turned out to be Lottie Ziegler, removed their helmets, puffing and panting. Mr. Reffell went to charge onto the stage but missed the first step, sending himself sprawling, much to the amusement of everyone in the room.

"Monty, you goose!" Mrs. Trimm roared.

The man dusted himself off and took to the microphone. "Oops, didn't realize Roman soldiers could be so clumsy," he said with a shrug. "Before I begin, can we have a round of applause for Miss Ziegler? A worthy opponent, indeed."

The children whistled and clapped and the woman took a bow.

"For heaven's sake, man, get on with it," Magoo hissed.

"Right, just a quick one," Mr. Reffell contin-ued. "I know lots of you are already signed up, but this is a tiny reminder that we're going to Rome in the New Year holiday and there are still a few spots left. All are welcome – as long as your parents pay, of course. Ha! Should be lots of fun – loads of history – so come and see me if you're interested."

The man turned and grinned at the headmaster, then hurried to take his seat at the staff table.

"Well, all that for not very much." Mr. MacGregor plastered on a smile. "Thank you, Mr. Reffell. I look forward to the feature-length film announcement you will no doubt bless us with next time."

Monty gave him the thumbs-up and another big grin.

"Is anyone allowed to go?" Max asked, as the children turned back to their lunch.

Carlos nodded. "I went to Greece last year – it was amazing. Reff is a bit bonkers, but he's a really good teacher. My parents can't wait to get rid of me again. I'm signed up. You should come too – if your parents let you."

"We've never been to Rome, even though

we've lived in Italy a couple of times," Max said.

He was half expecting one of the kids to ask him more about their life and was surprised when no one said a word.

Kensy looked across at her brother, then she saw Amelie sitting at the next table. At the mention of parents, the girl swiftly turned her head. Kensy made a mental note to tell Max what Amelie had said earlier – she was sure there was more to it than the girl was prepared to let on.

CHAPTER 29

JOP YOFDEQPFAB

The children hopped out of the taxi, which was parked against the curb at number thirteen. True to his word, Song had been waiting outside their school to whisk them straight home. Kensy had managed to grab a minute with her brother on their way to the front gates and had told him about Amelie's peculiar behavior and what the girl had said about their parents. Max thought it odd too, especially as he confirmed that neither of them had told anyone what was going on.

"Are you going to Mrs. Brightside's?" Max asked as he followed Kensy upstairs.

"I suppose. Do you want to come with me?" she asked.

Max nodded. "Sure. I'll just get changed."

The boy walked into his immaculate room and quickly got out of his uniform, hanging it up in the wardrobe. He selected a pair of dark jeans and a red checked shirt with a light-blue sweater over the top and boat shoes.

Kensy hurried to get changed as well, although her school clothes only made it as far as being flung over her chair. She chose a light-blue pair of jeans and a purple striped sweater, then tied another pink top around her waist and donned a pair of red sneakers. The rest of her clothes had miraculously returned to the wardrobe. She'd have to remember to thank Song later.

"What do you think it is?" Max asked from the doorway, startling Kensy, who was holding the envelope. She dropped it onto the floor. As she bent down to pick it up, she realized that it had a small tear in the corner. "Oh great, if we give it back to her now, she'll think we've been snooping. So we might as well."

Before Max could protest, Kensy ripped open the envelope and emptied its contents onto her desk. There was a round disc and another small black rectangular object with unmarked buttons on it.

"Well, that's not worth the ire of Mrs. Brightside, is it?" Max said. "I'll get another envelope." He opened the top drawer of Kensy's desk and located one the right size. He wrote "E. B." to match the original.

"What do you think they're for?" the girl mused.

"Looks like a fob to get into a building."

"She probably has a gymnastics studio somewhere." The girl grinned, imagining Mrs. Brightside leaping about in her leopard-print leotard. She dropped the items into the new envelope and sealed it. "Come on, let's head over. I'd hate for her to miss her classes."

"We'd better let Song know or he'll have a heart attack when he can't find us," Max said. "I'll tell him."

The boy ran ahead of his sister, making his way downstairs to the entrance hall then down again to the basement kitchen, where the butler was chopping carrots and zucchini at a hand-blurring speed while singing along to an upbeat country melody.

Max marveled at the man's skills. "Whoa, how do you do that?"

Song looked up and waved the knife in the air. "A great deal of practice," he said, raising his left eyebrow. "Would you like afternoon tea, Master Maxim? I have made a humming-bird cake and it is delicious, even if I do say so myself."

"Sounds great, but I'll have some when we come back. Kensy and I are going over to see Mrs. Brightside for a minute," the boy said. "Kensy saw her drop an envelope and we need to give it back to her."

"Oh, I will come with you then," Song said. He slid the vegetables from the chopping board into a saucepan full of water on the unlit cooktop.

"You really don't need to," Max protested. "How much trouble can we get into walking from one side of the street to the other?

Okay, don't answer that. But, seriously, we'll be fine."

Song pondered for a moment and rubbed his chin. "I do need to get the leg of lamb into the oven or we will be eating at midnight . . . How about I just watch you cross the road?"

He removed his apron and hung it on a hook near the door, then followed Max upstairs, where Kensy was waiting.

"You don't need to come," she said, eyeing Song. "You said that Mrs. Brightside was lovely, so now we're going to see whether you were telling the truth."

Song opened the front door and walked into the middle of the street like a crossing guard, ready to stop any cars that came along. Kensy and her brother grinned and rolled their eyes at one another.

"You know you're being ridiculous," Max said, glancing left and right. There wasn't a moving vehicle in sight.

"One cannot be too careful," the butler replied. His eyes darted all over the place as he made sure nothing was out of the ordinary.

"The only person acting suspiciously around here, Song, is you," Kensy said. She walked up the gutter to the sidewalk opposite while the butler headed back to the town house. "We're just going to push the envelope through the slot."

"We should at least see if she's home," Max said. "Otherwise she won't know you were the good Samaritan who found it."

Kensy groaned, but gave in and knocked tentatively on the door.

"Well, no one's going to hear that," Max said. He grasped the door knocker in the shape of a lion's head and gave it a firm belt.

The children waited for a full minute. Kensy was about to drop the envelope through the letter box in the door when a voice echoed from inside. The girl's stomach dropped.

"Hold your horses, I'm comin'!" Esme Brightside howled, shortly before opening the front door.

"Hello, Mrs. B.," Song called from the doorway of number thirteen. "The children found something that belongs to you. Could you please see to it they return home safely as I must attend to my lamb?"

The old woman flashed him a smile. "Are you doin' a roast for dinner?"

Song nodded.

The old woman licked her lips. "Oh, that sounds delicious. I can't remember the last time I 'ad a roast. When it's just me, it's 'ardly worth the effort." She looked downcast and sighed.

"I am sure that we will have more than enough for one extra. I will bring you a plate," Song promised.

"Oh, Song darlin', you are too kind. Thank you, my lovely." Mrs. Brightside gave the man a wave before he hurried inside, then turned to Kensy and Max. She scrunched up her nose and narrowed her eyes. "Now, what 'ave you possibly got that belongs to me?"

Kensy and Max gulped in unison. Mrs. Brightside didn't seem quite as lovely right now.

The telephone rang inside. The woman danced around for a few seconds, as if deciding whether or not to answer it. "Come in then," she ordered, indicating for the children to follow her. "And shut the door behind you."

Esme appeared to forget she used a cane when she scurried into the sitting room and picked up the telephone that was sitting on the arm of a tatty lounge chair.

"No," she barked. "Garnet, you never listen. I've already told you. LAX on Saturday. Call me back in 'alf an 'our when I might feel more inclined to speak to you." She hung up the phone and exhaled loudly before turning back to the children. "Sorry about that. Just my idiot 'usband. So, where is it, this thing of mine?"

Kensy wondered if the woman's husband was always the subject of such abuse. She took a deep breath and began to explain. "We were at the Graff Exhibition this morning with our class when the fire alarm went off. I think you must have dropped this," Kensy said, pulling the envelope from her jeans pocket.

Esme Brightside's eyes lit up and she rushed toward Kensy, grabbing it from her hands and clutching it to her chest. She held it out again and stared at it, as if it were the most precious jewel in the world. "I . . . I didn't realize. I thought it was in me bag. That'll teach me for using it as a filin' cabinet. Oh, you clever girl. I'd have been in a bit of bother if you 'adn't found that." She hugged Kensy tightly.

Max cowered, hoping he wasn't about to meet a similar fate.

"Angel child." Esme beamed as little flecks of white spittle gathered in the wrinkles at the corners of her mouth.

Max looked around the sitting room. It was not nearly as glamorous as Dame Spencer's town house across the road. The decor was comprised of old net curtains and a garish floral carpet. The mismatched and somewhat threadbare velvet lounge chairs had seen better days too. Unlike Dame Spencer's open-plan layout, this house was divided into much smaller rooms and there was a horrible smell – mildew coupled with sardines, perhaps.

The boy noticed a stack of travel brochures on the coffee table with pictures of beautiful crystal-clear waters and sandy beaches. The one on top advertised the splendors of the Dominican Republic.

"Come through to the kitchen – I've got somefin' for you," the woman said. Mrs. Brightside picked up her cane that was leaning against the wall and shuffled into the grimy hallway.

The children followed her past a staircase to the back of the house, the carpet crunching underfoot with dirt and grit. Clearly, Mrs. Brightside wasn't fond of vacuuming – unlike Song, who did it every day.

Tucked into the rear of the ground floor was a pocket-sized space with an old electric range, a dull steel sink and a few cupboards with chipped countertops and bright-yellow doors. There was a laminate table in the center of the room with two chairs upholstered in orange vinyl. A naked light bulb worked hard to illuminate the space.

Mrs. Brightside reached up and pulled a rusted biscuit tin from one of the cupboards. Max wondered if it was full of money. He'd heard stories about old people who didn't trust banks and kept their fortunes in tins or under their mattresses.

The woman pried open the lid, disturbing a plume of dust. She retrieved two small packets of biscuits, like the ones you'd get at a motel with the tea and coffee. Max didn't mind the shortbread variety but, given the dust, they had to have been there for a while.

"One for you and one for you," she said, handing a packet to each twin. "I don't know what you really 'ad to do with any of this, but you're a nice-lookin' young lad."

"Oh, I don't expect anything, Mrs. Brightside," the boy replied.

"What, my biscuits not good enough for you?" She looked at him accusingly. "And 'ere I was thinkin' you 'ad such good manners for a boy."

"No, they're my favorite, thank you," Max backtracked, lest the old lady find her handbag within reach and belt him over the head with it.

The woman shooed them with her hand. "Well, off you go then. I've got packin' to do."

"Are you going on holiday?" Kensy asked.

"Somefin' like that," the woman said.

Kensy turned around to leave just as the front door opened and Derek's voice echoed down the hall.

"Es, I'm back," he called.

Esme sprinted past the twins to intercept him. "Mind your language! I've got visitors," she shouted.

"Hiya, kids," Derek said, giving them a wave from the hallway. "We're old friends. I drove 'em to school this mornin'."

"You wait in the kitchen until I say goodbye to the children," Esme said, nodding her head in that direction.

"Bye, Derek," Max said. "And thanks again for the lift." But Derek didn't move. He stood in the hallway watching the children.

"Why would 'e 'ave to drive you to Central London Free? Is there somefin' wrong wiv your legs?" Esme asked.

Kensy was dying to ask her the same thing, as whatever ailed her seemed to come and go in the blink of an eye. She couldn't help herself.

"Mrs. Brightside, are you a gymnast, by any chance?"

Esme turned and looked at the girl as if she'd just been slapped with a wet fish. "I'm seventy-nine years old, lovey. I 'ave a bent back and a bad 'ip. Do I look like a gymnast?"

Kensy shook her head. "It's just that the other night I thought I saw someone in your upstairs room leaping about and doing handstands and cartwheels and the splits."

"You must have been lookin' at the house next door because, I can assure you, it weren't me," the old woman tutted.

"But you were a champion when you was a girl," Derek piped up. "Me mam told me you was in the Olympics."

"Didn't I tell you to wait in the kitchen?" Esme said, glaring at the lad. She turned back to the twins. "If only I 'ad such agility nowadays, but look at me. Old age is a terrible fing. Anyway, you'd better be off or Song'll be worryin'."

The children were practically pushed out onto the street. Esme reminded them to get

Song to deliver the roast, then promptly shut the door. Glad to get away, Kensy and Max made their way across the street and came face-to-face with Claudia pushing her pram.

"Hi there," the woman said, looking pleased to see them. "Are your knees better, Kensington?"

The girl nodded. "Yes, thank you."

Claudia pointed at number fourteen. "Did I see you come out of Mrs. Brightside's place?"

Kensy explained they were returning something the woman had lost.

"Is your baby awake today?" Max asked. He really did have a huge soft spot for little ones and would have loved to see her.

Claudia shook her head. "She's just gone to sleep, so please don't wake her or I'll be up all night." The woman looked as if she was about to set off again when she hesitated. "What's it like in there?" she said, gesturing to Mrs. Brightside's place. "I'm thinking about doing some renovations myself and I wondered what she's been up to. That young lad with the fancy car has been bringing so much rubble out I thought she must be tearing the place apart."

"Oh no, it's really old and dingy," Max said, wrinkling his nose. "I don't think she's doing renovations unless it's in the cellar. If you want to see a lovely makeover, you should come and have a look at Dame Spencer's house. It's beautiful."

It was getting to that time of the evening when commuters were walking home and several well-dressed men and women trotted along the sidewalk.

"We'd better go," Kensy said, before saying goodbye, but Claudia didn't reply. She looked to be deep in thought.

Kensy and Max walked up to number thirteen and rang the buzzer. Song released the door latch from the kitchen, then charged upstairs to meet the children in the hall.

"How was Mrs. Brightside?" he asked, glad to see they were back safe and sound.

"She gave us this as a reward," Kensy replied, and thrust the packet of two biscuits toward the butler.

He considered the cloudy packaging with a look of distaste. "I think perhaps they will go into the bin, seeing that the expiry date is four years ago. I suppose she meant well."

"She's weird," Max said, closing the front door behind him. "I feel sorry for her husband."

"Oh, Mrs. Brightside does not have a husband. He left her some time ago," Song said.

"Well, that's strange because she was talking to him on the telephone when we were there," Kensy said. "And she wasn't very nice to him at all."

"I think she might be a bit of a Jekyll and Hyde character," Max said. "And don't ask us to take over her dinner – you can do that all on your own."

Song smiled. "She will be grateful, but I hope she doesn't give me any biscuits as a reward. Please come downstairs, children. I have some news."

Kensy grabbed her brother's hand. "Is it Mum and Dad?" she said, her heart in her throat.

"Come," the man said, and led the way down to the kitchen, where the aroma of roasting lamb filled the air. Wellie and Mac hopped out of their beds and leapt onto Kensy and Max's laps as soon as they sat at the kitchen table, where Song had already placed two small slices of hummingbird cake and two hot chocolates.

"Song, stop stalling. What is it?" Kensy demanded.

"Kens, calm down. He's going to tell us," Max remonstrated. He looked at the butler. "What is it, Song?"

Song sat down at the end of the table with a heavy air. "I have news from Mr. Fitz, but I am afraid it is not what you have been hoping for."

CHAPTER 30

ZIRB

Although Kensy and Max wanted more than anything for Fitz to have found their parents, that wasn't the case, but they weren't giving up – there was no reason to. They just couldn't tell Song why they hadn't fallen apart. The twins knew their mother and father were safe somewhere and that everything would be all right as soon as Fitz got back and they could tell him what they knew. There would also be some serious questions about whether Fitz even went to Africa in the first place.

That night, over dinner, Song had regaled them with tales of his childhood growing up with Sidney in Shanghai. As boys, they had often played tricks on their parents and teachers, given they were almost impossible to tell apart. Coupled with their unusual height, the pair had always attracted a lot of attention, though they didn't particularly enjoy it. Their father and grandfather had both been butlers for wealthy English merchants in the city, and so it was the family business that Song and his brother had fallen into when they moved to London in their early twenties.

"I did not tell Sidney that I had applied for a job with Sir Dominic and he did not tell me that he had done so as well," Song confided. "We both got the job and wondered if Sir Dominic was confused and thought we were the same person!"

Kensy's brows furrowed. "Who's Sir Dominic?"

"Is that Dame Spencer's husband?" Max asked. "There was a picture of him in the corridor near her office. He looked like . . . Never mind,

I'm sure it's just a coincidence."

"Confucius says coincidences are like meeting places in the universe," Song said.

Kensy looked at her brother. "Do you think that's true?"

Max shrugged. "Hard to tell. But I'll check it out later."

"Oh no, do not trouble yourself," Song said, waving a hand in the air. Wellie and Mac raised their heads and barked.

"He definitely made it up," Kensy said to Max.

The boy laughed. "Even the dogs know when you're telling fibs, Song."

Kensy grinned at the butler. "You know, you're a bit weird, but you're pretty funny."

"Thank you, Miss Kensington," Song replied, his eyes twinkling. "Perhaps we should play a game after dinner, as long as you don't have any homework. Scrabble or Cluedo?"

Kensy and Max glanced at each other. "Cluedo!" they answered in unison.

Song chuckled and clapped his hands. "Splendid choice. I, too, love a good mystery."

CHAPTER 31

HFAKXMMBA

Max woke on Friday morning missing his parents so much it made his chest ache. He checked his watch and, finding nothing, picked up the book he'd been reading. Anything to distract his thoughts. It was from the shelf in his room – a crime thriller that, despite recent events, he found himself enjoying. As he flipped open the pages, Max noticed a newspaper clipping tucked into the middle of it. He unfolded the cutting to reveal an old photograph.

Max sat up, his heart pounding once he realized exactly what it was. He slowly replayed the events of the past few days in his mind like a movie. So many things hadn't been adding up, but now seeing this, a lot more of them did. He resisted the urge to show Kensy, unsure if she was quite ready for this much truth. After all, it seemed that they'd been lied to for the past eleven years. He'd tell her later when the time was right.

With the weight of the world on his shoulders, the boy hopped out of bed, showered and dressed for school, tucking the clipping safely into his blazer pocket. He went down to breakfast and munched on his toast in silence, trying to work out when to tell Kensy about the photograph. He had always been terrible at keeping things from his twin sister. Kensy appeared to be distracted too and had dark circles under her eyes. She'd hardly slept again and didn't even object when Song put on a country ballad and hummed along, though he did so without his usual enthusiasm.

Song insisted that they were driving to school again, but just before the group was due to leave the house, he received a call that altered their plans.

"I am sorry, children," the butler said, as he slipped his phone into his pocket and ushered the pair through the front door. "I am afraid Dame Spencer requires me for an urgent errand. My brother is attending to something of equal importance – can you believe that there are times one butler is simply not enough?"

Max grinned and buttoned his coat. "I'd have thought one butler would be plenty. Don't worry, Song. We'll be fine. School is just two minutes away and at least your driver is here on time today."

A taxi had just puttered to a stop in front of number thirteen as Kensy followed her brother outside. This morning the sky looked as though a gray blanket had fallen to Earth and tucked itself into every nook and cranny.

Song leaned in through the open passenger window and spoke briefly to the driver, who grunted a reply as the children clambered into the back. The butler tapped on the window and gave the children a wave. He watched the cab drive away, turning right at the corner.

Kensy fastened her seat belt and plonked her bag on the floor. "I'm going to see Mrs. Vanden Boom about my watch first thing," she said, yawning. "I want it back, whether she's managed to find a way into it or not."

The taxi drove past Mrs. Grigsby standing outside her shop.

"She looks different today," the boy observed aloud. The woman was wearing a floral dress with stockings and heeled shoes. Her frizzy hair had been tamed into soft curls and she almost looked as if she were smiling.

"Perhaps she's leaving for the Caribbean," Kensy said. "Wouldn't that be good? Hopefully, whoever has bought the shop doesn't eat small children for breakfast."

Max frowned. "That's weird. Did you see that Mrs. Brightside also had travel brochures? Perhaps they're going away together."

"Song did say they were good friends," the girl reasoned. "Although I can't imagine anyone being friends with Mrs. Grigsby and, if you ask me, there's something not right with Mrs. Brightside either. She's got secrets."

Max thought about his own secret that was burning a hole in his trouser pocket and debated with himself about whether to say anything. The taxi made a left turn and then a right, but instead of stopping at the school gates, the driver sped up. Max knocked politely on the plastic screen that divided driver and passenger. "Excuse me, sir, that was our school back there. Can you please stop and let us out?"

Without a word or any sign of acknowledgment, the driver pressed his foot on the accelerator. The children gasped as they were thrown backward against the seat.

Kensy's stomach tightened. "Max," she whispered, grabbing her brother's arm, "what's happening?"

The boy swallowed hard. "I don't know."

Kensy spotted Harper walking along the street. She banged on the taxi window in an attempt to get the girl's attention, but Harper looked straight through her. Kensy fiddled with the button to put the window down, but it wouldn't budge. Max tried the door handle on his side of the vehicle to find it was also locked.

"Not so clever now, are you?" the driver said menacingly through the speaker.

Kensy and Max looked at each other in bewilderment.

"What do you mean?" Max demanded.

"Let's just say that not everyone's so pleased to see you two," the man said.

Kensy flinched. There was something about that gravelly voice. She'd heard it before at Alexandria! She peered at the man through the clear barrier, but he didn't look remotely familiar.

"What have we done?" Max asked him. "We're just kids."

Up ahead a police car swerved into the road, its sirens wailing. The taxi driver made a quick right turn into the street that ran toward the rear of the Tate Gallery but was confronted by more police vehicles. He performed a U-turn and headed in the direction they'd come from only to find another police cordon. The taxi driver grunted and turned back toward the gallery; this time the fellow had no choice but to stop at the police checkpoint. He pushed a button in the center console just as an officer tapped on the driver's window. He put it down, but not very far.

"We're stopping all vehicles as a precaution-ary measure," the policeman said. "There's been a robbery."

The children yelled out and waved at him in desperation, but it was as if the car had tinting so dark that no one could see inside. Kensy was utterly confounded. Surely the policeman only had to turn his head and he would notice them through the plastic screen. The girl reached into her bag and pulled out her plastic ruler.

Max looked at her. "What are you doing with that?"

"You'll see," the girl said, and attempted to shove it through the money tray. Except the ruler jammed against thin air, as if there were some sort of invisible seal preventing it from reaching the driver's side of the partition. Kensy felt as though she'd swallowed a handful of sand; her worst fears had been confirmed.

Max, meanwhile, was trying to break his window. He even slammed his bag against it, but to no effect.

Kensy swiveled around and began feeling along the back seats for a release button. There had to be one. Bingo! The girl lifted it up and the seat dropped forward. Kensy clambered into the tiny trunk space cramped with a spare wheel and some tools.

"Max, get me a paper clip," she hissed, but her brother was two steps ahead and had already located one in his pencil case. Kensy fiddled with the lock and managed to pop open the trunk within seconds. "Quick! We've got to go now!"

As the engine roared to life, the twins rolled out of the back of the taxi onto the roadway behind.

Kensy gasped, pointing at the two heads in the rear window. "It looks like there are people in there!"

"It's a hologram. That's why the policeman couldn't see us!" Max said.

They watched the taxi disappear around the corner, the driver apparently oblivious to the loss of his cargo. The policeman who had stopped them had walked across to the other side of the street and was having an animated conversation with an elderly gentleman. The children got to their feet and ran toward the museum. Surely someone there could help them.

CHAPTER 32

QEB MBXZLZH

Kensy and Max barreled toward a uniformed officer who was stationed outside the police tape surrounding the side entrance of the Tate Gallery.

"Please can you help us?" the boy puffed.

The officer eyed them warily. "What's happened?"

"We were just kidnapped by a man driving a black cab. The whole back was a capsule and we could see out, but no one could see in," the boy said, struggling to catch his breath. "We were stopped at a checkpoint around the corner and we managed to escape through the trunk."

The young constable chuckled. "Okay, James Bond, I think you and your girlfriend had better be getting to school. We don't have time for pranks. Someone disabled the security system and the Graff Peacock's been stolen. It's worth a fortune and no one saw them go in or out. Sounds like a tunnel job, if you ask me. But then you two could probably solve the crime, couldn't you – given what you've imagined just happened?"

"Oh for goodness' sake," Max shouted. "Why is everyone in London out to get us?"

Kensy looked at her brother, her mouth opening and closing like a goldfish. Was this really her coolheaded twin talking?

The police officer rolled his eyes. "Good one, kid. You should be an actor, you know."

Max took a few deep breaths then turned to his sister. "Sorry, I don't know what got into me."

With sinking hearts, the children realized they were getting absolutely nowhere with this fellow and decided the only thing to do was to go home and tell Song. He'd believe them. The twins took off, thinking it was probably safest to take the main road, although the mere sight of a black cab almost sent Kensy skyward.

"Who do you think that guy was and what did he want with us?" Max said, as they dashed past another police cordon. Traffic was building up as drivers were questioned and redirected.

Kensy shook her head. "It must have something to do with Mum and Dad. All of this weirdness began with their disappearance."

The kids charged past The Morpeth Arms, which hadn't yet opened, and were nearing Ponsonby Terrace when Claudia appeared around the corner. Max almost ran straight into the pram she was pushing and only just managed to stop himself in time.

"My gosh, you two," Claudia said, looking concerned. "What's happened? Shouldn't you be at school?"

"We were kidnapped by a taxi driver, but the silly policeman didn't believe us," Kensy blurted. "We've got to find Song."

Claudia's eyes widened in disbelief. "What

do you mean you were kidnapped?"

Max quickly filled her in on the details. Unlike the young constable, though, the woman hung on to his every word.

"And the Peacock Brooch has been stolen from the Tate," Max added. "We only saw it yesterday."

Kensy's mind was racing. She was thinking about Mrs. Brightside and those gadgets she and Max had returned to her last night. She looked at Max and Max looked at her.

"Mrs. Brightside!" the children gasped in unison.

"She hasn't been renovating," Kensy said slowly.

Max nodded. "She's been tunneling."

"What?" Claudia's brows appeared ready to leap off her forehead.

"It was Mrs. Brightside and the other lady who works at the gallery and Derek Grigsby," Max said. "*They* took the Peacock Brooch."

Talking at the speed of light, Kensy relayed their visit to the Tate and the contents of the envelope addressed to Esme Brightside. "I knew that old lady was full of secrets! Those gadgets in the envelope were probably for the alarms and cameras," the girl said, "and it was that other woman who works there who gave them to her. No wonder she was so happy I'd returned them."

"And Derek hasn't been renovating – he's been digging!" Max exclaimed. "I'd put money on him having found a tunnel from the old prison that goes straight to the gallery. That's how they've done it. This whole area is riddled with them. Gary at the pub told us."

"Esme Brightside might be ancient, but she's tricky," Kensy told Claudia, who was looking more incredulous by the second. "I saw her through the curtains one night doing flips and jumps. I bet it was her who got the jewel. And, Max, remember how Derek said she was an Olympic gymnast when she was young?"

Claudia put her wrist to her mouth and spoke so quickly the children didn't catch what she said or what exactly she was doing. "They've probably already left the country, but notify the airports anyway," the woman finished.

Max recalled the brochures splayed across Esme Brightside's coffee table. "They're heading for the Dominican Republic, to be precise."

Kensy nodded. "And their husbands are meeting them at LAX. That's the international airport in Los Angeles."

Claudia's face drained of color. The poor woman looked as if she was about to faint. "I've been on this case for over a year and two eleven-year-olds have solved it," she wheezed. "I'll be sacked for sure."

It was the children's turn to look surprised.

"Who do you work for?" Max asked.

Claudia pointed across the river.

"You're MI6?" he said, his eyes wide. Max gestured to the pram. "There's no baby, is there?"

Claudia shook her head and lifted the covering on the pram to reveal a doll and a transmitter that made baby noises.

"So that's why you weren't keen for me to have a look," Max said, a grin creeping on to his face. "That's really cool."

"Not if I let them get away." The woman's shoulders slumped. "It's bad enough we lost

Garnet Brightside, Walter Grigsby and Ray Daggett a year and a half ago. The three old geezers pulled off the greatest diamond heist in history before skipping town, and I've been watching their wives for a year, hoping they would lead us to them. And now you've gone ahead and cracked the case."

"Come on, let's go," Kensy urged. "They might still be around."

Claudia didn't need to be told twice. She took off up the road, abandoning the pram on the sidewalk. Max hesitated, thinking an unattended pram would attract far too much attention. He grabbed the handle and the three of them tore around the corner with Claudia speaking into her sleeve the whole way. They pulled up sharply at the sight of Derek standing beside his blinged-up hatchback with the driver's door open. His mother was in the back seat with Ivy Daggett, who Claudia identified as the lady who worked at the Tate Gallery.

Claudia and the children approached silently, getting close enough to hear what they were saying.

"'Urry up, Esme!" Wanda called. "The ship'll

leave without us."

"Did she just say a ship?" Claudia whispered. "Didn't you hear Esme tell her husband that she was meeting him at LAX?"

Kensy nodded.

Claudia whispered into her sleeve. "On my signal . . ."

"Oh, put a sock in it, Wanda!" Esme grouched, closing her front door. "You'd better not start – we're a long time gettin' there and a long time gone, if you don't remember."

"I wish I could see the look on Dad's face when 'e realizes we're not meetin' 'em." Derek grinned his shiny smile. "Serves 'em right for leavin' us and gamblin' away all the money. That's a very good idea, callin' the FBI once we're safely away. That'll show the old geezers who can really pull off an 'eist. And it doesn't 'urt that I'm a genius that worked out the Dominican Republic 'as no extradition treaty wiv England."

Esme threw her walking stick onto the ground and practically catapulted herself into the passenger seat.

"Go!" Claudia shouted.

The children were stunned to see agents appear from everywhere, surrounding the vehicle with their weapons drawn.

"Sorry, kids, I've got to run," Claudia said, and charged off to lead the arrest.

A silver van hurtled into the street followed by a tow truck and, within less than a few minutes, the four thieves were gone and Derek's blingy hatchback with them.

CHAPTER 33

CFQW

Max and Kensy were still reeling from the fact that they had just cracked Britain's greatest diamond heist and another jewel theft that would undoubtedly go down in the annals of history. Pity no one would ever know about it.

The children crossed the road to number thirteen, but just as Kensy was about to hit the buzzer, Max grabbed her hand. He shook his head and pointed at the silhouette in the top-right window. "That's not Song. They're too bulky."

"What if he's in there and he's been hurt?" Kensy whispered. "Shouldn't we try to help?"

Max heard footsteps just inside. He motioned to his sister and the pair leapt over the balcony railing and down to the basement entrance below, where they huddled under the steps. The front door opened and footfalls sounded on the walkway above. The twins held their breath.

"No, the butler's not 'ere and the kids aren't either," a man growled. "'Ow on earth did you lose them out of the back of the taxi, you blinkin' bozo? The boss will not be 'appy."

Max squinted through a small gap between the step treads but could only see the back of the man's head. He appeared to be talking on his phone.

"We'll meet back at HQ. Might 'ave to lie low for a while," the man continued, and hurried across the sidewalk, where he hopped into the driver's seat of a black cab.

Kensy waited until the vehicle disappeared around the end of the road near the Thames before he spoke. "Do you think all the taxi drivers in London are bad guys?" she breathed.

Max shook his head. "I don't know, but let's

go to the *Beacon*. I'm pretty sure Dame Spencer can help us."

The pair ran up the steps and along the road in the opposite direction to the taxi. They didn't stop until they reached the newspaper's offices. Luckily, the security guard recognized them from their previous visit and let them straight through. They skidded across the polished floor to the reception desk.

"Please, we need to see Dame Spencer," Max panted.

The young woman smiled at them brightly. "I'm terribly sorry, but she's not available at the moment. I can take a message."

"But we *have* to see her," Kensy insisted. "It's a matter of life-and-death."

The woman gave the eleven-year-old twins a look not dissimilar to that of the policeman outside the Tate. She held up a finger as she turned away to answer the phone. Kensy, noticing people coming and going via the staff entrance, nudged her brother and pointed. Without a moment's hesitation, they tailgated two young fellows through to the other side.

Max spotted a harried-looking man carrying a stack of papers coming out of the stairwell. "Quick!" he said, sprinting toward it. He slid his foot inside just before it clanked shut. "Ow," he complained, rubbing his ankle.

The pair charged upstairs. Once they reached the thirteenth floor, the twins peered around the door. When all was clear, they slipped out and found themselves at the far end of the hallway to Dame Spencer's office. They ran for it, their feet thudding and squeaking against the marble floor.

"Max!" Kensy gasped, skidding to a halt. She pointed to the portrait of Dominic Spencer. "He looks like Dad."

Max reached into his blazer pocket and pulled out the newspaper clipping he'd found that morning. "I was going to say that the last time we were here, but Sidney interrupted us," he said, and held out the clipping for her to see.

Kensy looked at the photograph of the well-dressed man and woman and the two young boys standing in front of them. "That's Dad," she said, frowning. "And Dame Spencer and that man on the wall . . . Are they . . .?"

Max nodded. "Think about it, Kens – the book at Alexandria. EDS, Edward, Dominic . . ."

"She's not in," a man said.

Kensy and Max spun around. "Fitz!" they cried, barreling toward him.

"I'm sorry I didn't find them," the man said. He shook his head and wiped the tears from Kensy's cheeks. "There's no trace."

When the children finally let go, they looked at one another, a silent agreement passing between them.

"Don't worry, Fitz. We know they're okay," Max said. "They sent us a message."

Fitz's brow furrowed. "How?"

Max patted his watch.

"Oh, thank heavens," Fitz said, and the twins could feel his relief.

"You can't tell anyone," Kensy said. "Mum and Dad were very clear. And you're the only person we can trust, although we're not even sure about that, considering how much you've lied to us."

Max crossed his arms, his eyes hardening. "Kensy saw you here when we came to meet Dame Spencer. I wasn't sure at the time, but it was you, wasn't it?"

Fitz exhaled. "Yes, but I can explain. That really doesn't matter now, but there's something else that does." He glanced down the hall at Cordelia Spencer's office.

"It's okay," Kensy said. "We know Dame Spencer is our grandmother."

Fitz's eyebrows jumped up in surprise. "Now, how did you two work that out?"

Kensy grinned, looking pleased with herself. "That portrait over there is a pretty good start. Max and Dad are the spitting image of Dominic Spencer, wouldn't you say?"

"I found a book at Alexandria with an inscription in code," Max added. "We worked it out. Even though the name wasn't exactly the same, I know it was Dad's."

"This confirmed it." Kensy held out the photograph Max had found that morning. "That's Dad, isn't it?"

"When we met Cordelia the other day, she wasn't exactly friendly and seemed to want nothing to do with us," Max said, looking into the man's gray eyes. "Why doesn't she want to know us? Did we do something bad?"

Fitz took a deep breath and shook his head. "Never. We've got a lot to talk about, but this isn't the place for it. Let's get you two back to school, or Magoo will be calling the police," he said, and ushered the children to the elevator. "I promise to tell you everything once we get there."

"Well, we've got some stories to tell you on the way too," Kensy said, and Max nodded.

CHAPTER 34

MEXOLP

Fitz listened while the twins explained everything that had happened that morning.

"You actually *need* to call the police," Kensy said, as they stepped out of the elevator and into a parking garage. "Someone tried to kidnap us *twice* and I think it was one of the groundskeepers from Alexandria – the one called Shugs. Well, it sounded like him, but the driver didn't look like anyone I've seen at the estate."

She gave Fitz a description of the driver's face and he said that it didn't match Shugs's features at all – and he'd known the man for years.

A black cab roared out of a spot and pulled up in front of them.

Kensy gulped. "The last time we hopped into one of those things we almost got killed," she said uneasily.

"I have no doubt that this one is perfectly safe," Fitz said, opening a passenger door. He gave Kensington a reassuring hug before jumping in ahead of them.

Kensy reluctantly followed suit, as did Max. The girl stared at the driver and was slightly comforted by the fact that he greeted the children with an Indian accent. The car popped out of the basement garage into a tiny side street and drove through a series of garages, the doors zipping up and down before they joined John Islip Street and headed for the school.

"What was that?" Max said, trying to get his head around what he'd just seen. Surely that wasn't normal.

Fitz flashed him a grin and a wink. "You'll see."

This time the car stopped at the school gates and the group got out. Fitz thanked the driver but didn't pay, which Max thought was a little odd.

Mrs. Potts gave the children a wave as they entered the building. It was strangely silent. "Mr. MacGregor will see you now," she trilled.

Fitz pushed open the door to the headmaster's study and found the man himself standing by a bookcase that was pivoted away from the wall.

"Hello, kids," Magoo said. "I hear you've had quite the adventure this morning, though I'm afraid there are a few more surprises to come."

Kensy looked at her brother and then at Fitz. "Good ones, I hope."

The children were taken into a narrow corridor past what appeared to be a full bathroom – and quite a glamorous one at that. The sight of a soggy pair of padded bicycle shorts hanging up next to the sink made Max smile. At the end of the bare concrete passage was an elevator, which they all piled into. Mr. MacGregor placed his palm on a black panel that lit up in green before the compartment rocketed downward. Max and Kensy looked at one another. This was definitely a bit different to the rest of Central London Free School.

When the doors opened, the twins discovered they were in another bare concrete corridor. One of the walls slid back and they were suddenly in a breathtaking room with high ceilings and elaborate cornicing. There was flocked green wallpaper and antiques of every description. If Max didn't know better, he would have guessed they were back at Alexandria.

Mr. MacGregor led them to a set of double doors. He pushed them open, exposing another enormous space, but this time the children were stunned to see several of their classmates and most of their teachers. There were two men Kensy realized were the police officers who had come to the town house after their first attempted kidnapping, as well as the taxi driver who had just dropped them off outside. Mim was also there, a warmth radiating from her weathered face. The room was lined with computers and other curious contraptions. There was a coat of arms bearing a name they'd never seen before, but one of the symbols was the same lighthouse that featured on the masthead of the *Beacon*. Mrs.

Vanden Boom smiled at the pair and waved, as did Mr. Reffell and Mrs. Trimm. Mr. Lazenby gave the children a sturdy nod.

Carlos and Autumn were there, as were Harper and Sachin, Yasmina, Inez, Dante and Alfie the rugby lad. There were some other children they recognized from school but didn't really know. Kensy spotted Amelie, who grinned sheepishly. Even Misha was there.

Kensy and Max looked around the room, their hearts pounding. "What is this place?" Max said.

The group parted down the center to reveal a huge desk and a high-backed chair facing away from them. There was a cabinet behind it heaving with books and various gadgets and gizmos. The chair spun around and the twins gasped.

"Dame Spencer!" they breathed in unison.

The woman stood up and walked around to the pair. "Actually, it's –"

"Granny Spencer," the twins chorused, and rushed toward her.

For a second, the woman was taken aback. Then she clung to the children as if her life depended on it. Finally, she let go of them and brushed tears from her eyes. Everyone else appeared to have an urgent need for tissues too and were pulling them from their pockets or, like Alfie, wiping their noses on their sleeves.

"I know you must have a million questions –" Cordelia began.

Max reached across and held his sister's hand. "Like who's trying to kill us for a start."

The woman took a deep breath. "Yes, well, they won't want to be anywhere near me when I find out." Dame Spencer's face hardened for a moment. "I suspect we have a double agent or two in our midst," she said, glancing toward Willow Witherbee, whose eyes hit the floor. "Our drivers are the most reliable in the world, though there are clearly a couple who are working to a different agenda."

Song and Sidney appeared carrying two fat leather-bound books, which they passed to the twins with a deep bow.

Kensy stared into her grandmother's green eyes – the same color as her own. "Are you a spy?" she asked. She looked around at everyone else in the room. "Are you all spies?"

Every head nodded up and down.

"So does that mean Derek Grigsby is a spy?" Max said, frowning. "He went to Central London Free School too."

Magoo MacGregor almost choked on his incredulity. "Oh good heavens, no. Could you imagine it? I believe you two have just had him locked up. Only a small number of our students are involved in the organization. It's part of their –" his eyes darted to Dame Spencer before he corrected himself – "*your* training. The majority of the children must never know, but all of the staff are on board."

"So you don't have singing lessons, then?" Kensy said, turning to Autumn.

The girl shook her head. "No, and that was a really dumb excuse. I'm completely tone-deaf. You would have found that out pretty quickly. Although I do play the piano."

Inez winced. "Ooh sorry, Autumn, I think I was the one who dropped you in it there."

Max grinned and pumped his fist. "Yes! I always knew there was something different about Mum and Dad and Fitz – I just could never put my finger on it."

"As if," Kensy scoffed, and caught Mrs. Vanden Boom's eye. "My watch? You said it looked just like an MK 13. What's that?"

The woman trembled from head to toe with excitement. "An incredible communications system that I was completely unaware existed outside of these walls," she fizzed. "But we can talk about that later."

"And the newspaper?" Max asked.

"Cover and coded messages," Fitz replied. "And the daily news."

Max looked at his long-lost grandmother. "Why haven't we ever known you? Mrs. Grigsby said that your son and his wife and cousin were killed in a plane crash – but that was Dad and Mum." He turned to Fitz. "Does that make you Dad's cousin? And, Mim, are you Granny's sister?"

"Sister-in-law," the woman said, her gray eyes glistening. "Your grandfather was my brother."

Fitz nodded. "I am your father's cousin and there's a lot to explain, but believe me when I say that your mum and dad have only ever wanted to protect you both."

"Did something bad happen?" Kensy asked. She couldn't think why else her parents would abandon their family and start a new life.

"Your parents just wanted you to have a normal existence," Fitz said.

Max raised his eyebrows. "By moving every six months and living in ski resorts all over the world? That's *so* normal – I mean, that's what most children do, isn't it?"

Fitz chuckled. "Yes, I see your point. It could have been worse, though. They might have worked for the tax office and opted for a quiet life in the suburbs."

"Mrs. Grigsby said that Dad has a brother," Kensy said, turning to her grandmother.

The woman smiled tightly. "That would be your Uncle Rupert. He's away at the moment. I imagine this news will be a little –" she paused, searching for the right words – "unsettling for him. You will meet in due time." Cordelia placed a hand on each of the children's shoulders. "Everything you need to know is contained within those pages. Welcome to Pharos, my darlings. You have just become part of the world's most secret and significant spy organization. Now, let's find your parents, shall we?"

THE CAESAR CIPHER

Named after Roman Emperor Julius Caesar, the Caesar cipher is a basic method for encrypting and decoding text. It involves moving the letters of the alphabet up or down by a fixed number of positions. The word "cipher" refers to a secret or disguised way of writing – a code of sorts.

For example, Julius Caesar shifted each letter of the text down by three positions and used this code in private correspondence. In this case, the letter A would become X, B becomes Y, C becomes Z and so on. The diagram below of the Caesar cipher will help you decode the chapter headings as well as the inscription in the book that Max discovered in the library.

A	B	C	D	E	F	G	H	I	J	K	L	M	N	O	P	Q	R	S	T	U	V	W	X	Y	Z
X	Y	Z	A	B	C	D	E	F	G	H	I	J	K	L	M	N	O	P	Q	R	S	T	U	V	W

There are many variations of the Caesar cipher, such as the Reverse Caesar cipher and another called the Vigenère cipher. You can do it too. Have a try by moving the bottom row of letters left or right to create your very own secret language!

ACKNOWLEDGEMENTS

Writing something new is incredibly exciting and more than a little nerve-racking. You want to get it right, and for me that means I need to be completely in love with my characters as well as the storyline. The characters of *Kensy and Max* have been brewing for a long time, but they needed to take shape and find a setting in which to have their adventures and that took a little longer. It's also been difficult to contemplate writing a new series while I'm still absolutely wedded to Alice-Miranda and Clementine Rose – but the girls have given me some leeway lately, and Kensy and Max have demanded my complete attention (until I write the next Alice-Miranda and Clemmie books).

This new series has been shaped by lots of people – not the least by my wonderful husband, Ian Harvey, who never complains when I want to bounce ideas around for hours, or when I ask him to read the manuscript over and over. He's undoubtedly my biggest fan and the best manager anyone could want or have. He's fabulous at the small details and I can't thank him enough for everything he does to support this somewhat crazy career of mine. I love you to the sun and stars and back again.

There are many other people to thank too, starting with the fabulous team at Penguin Random House Australia: my publisher, Holly Toohey, who always takes my calls, listens to my mad ideas and never fails to make me think I can do this; my editor, Catriona Murdie, who is clever and pedantic and challenges me to be better every single time and does it all in the nicest way possible; the superstar marketing and publicity team so ably led by Dot Tonkin, with a special mention to Zoe Bechara, my publicist extraordinaire; Jen Harris, Tina Gumnior, Kate Sheahan and Suz Katris (before she went to the dark side!); head of sales, Angela Duke; the rights team led by Nerrilee Weir; Eleanor Shorne Holden and Vicki Grundy; the lovely Laura Harris, publishing director for Young Readers; and the fabulous Julie Burland, whose leadership is inspiring and whose friendship is greatly valued – that you find the best people and provide so many opportunities for them to shine is testament to why you're the "Big Boss."

I must give special thanks to my brilliant illustrator, Anne Yi, with whom I have now done 30 books. Anne is one of those incredibly talented people who can take a description and turn it into something wonderful. I adore how she has brought Kensy and Max to life. And to our designer, Christa Moffitt – thank you, the cover is fabulous.

I also need to thank a very special group of readers who have been with me along the way – some from the very beginning and others more recently. To Toby Cox, Georgia Cameron, Linda Cameron, Georgie Mallyon, Denae Vanderplas and Justine Wallis, thank you for being my first readers, for telling me the bits you loved (and liked not so much) and for ultimately helping me to shape the book into something I hope lots of kids are going to want to read.

Heartfelt thanks to my family and friends, my readers, all the parents, librarians, teachers and booksellers who have championed my books and given me so much encouragement to write *Kensy and Max*. I also want to thank the real Gary, from The Morpeth Arms in Millbank, for taking me on that tour of the cells and telling me all about the spies and, in doing so, giving me the idea for where to set the first book. Huge thanks to Dame Gail Rebuck, former CEO of Random House UK, for being a wonderful supporter of my work and inviting me up to her office in Vauxhall Bridge Road, which unexpectedly provided me with another perfect location and perhaps some inspiration for another very special dame.

And to Kensy and Max, may you head out into the world and find readers who fall in love with you as much as I have.

Jacqueline Harvey

ABOUT THE AUTHOR

Jacqueline Harvey taught for many years in girls' boarding schools. She is the author of the bestselling Alice-Miranda series and the Clementine Rose series, and was awarded Honor Book in the 2006 Australian CBC Awards for her picture book *The Sound of the Sea*. She now writes full time and is working on more Alice-Miranda, Clementine Rose, and Kensy and Max adventures.

jacquelineharvey.com.au

Read Them All!